D0865834

KING CROW

KING CROW

Michael Stewart

Bluemoose

First published in 2011 by
Bluemoose Books Ltd
25 Sackville Street
Hebden Bridge
West Yorkshire
HX7 7DJ

Reprinted 2012, 2020

www.bluemoosebooks.com

British Library Cataloguing-in-Publication data
A catalogue record for this book is available from the-British-Library

Hardback   ISBN 13: 978-0-956687616

Paperback ISBN 13: 978-0-956687609

Printed and bound in the UK by Short Run Press, Exeter

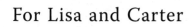

For Lisa and Carter

Starlings

When I look at people, I wonder what sort of birds they are. A photograph of the headmaster, Mr Hulmes, stares down from the display board. His profile reminds me of a long-eared owl, with his large round face and flat nose, bushy eyebrows like the erect blackish ear-tufts of the bird.

Perhaps I've studied the board too long because when I turn round, I'm on my own. I get to the end of the corridor and I'm confronted by a gang of boys and girls. One of the girls is dragging another girl by her hair across the floor. The girl must be about twelve. I turn back, but now some of the gang are behind me. I'm trapped.

I watch as they kick the girl. One of them films it on his phone. Her pleading eyes, her mouth like a gash of fear. Kick, kick, kick. What now? Finches. Focus on finches. Come on, think. The goldfinch. Think about the goldfinch. I think the goldfinch is one of the prettiest birds in the world. The European goldfinch I'm talking about. I've seen American goldfinches in books and they're nothing like as pretty – yellow and black rather than gold. Not that the European goldfinch is really gold, it's not gold at all, but the combination of red face, black and white head and yellow and black wings is very striking. I have a special seed feeder to attract them in the yard, although, as we have just moved in, I've not yet succeeded there. Shame really, because by the time we left the last place there were swarms of them, regular as clockwork.

Block out the girl. Teachers, where are they? I imagine Mr Hulmes swooping down, silent, grasping the predators. The girl tries to cover her face with her hands. Where are the teachers?

What other finches have I seen? Well, obviously greenfinch and chaffinch. I see them all the time. When we lived the other side of Salford, towards Ordsall Park, we used to get quite a few hawfinch. Not that many really. Hardly any at all. Well, none. When we went to Bangor a few years ago, before mum got with Tina and we went on holidays, I'm sure I saw a twite. Never seen a rosefinch or a redpoll – but I live in hope. The fight, the noise. Keep thinking finches. Scarlet rosefinch, mottled brown with streaked breast. And that rose colour, almost red. I like the finches very much. I like their bills – they all have good short, strong bills. Very well adapted for eating seeds.

This boy swaggers over. He has hair like straw and grey eyes. Navy blue, white, crimson tie. The ringleader.

—Face on him, he says. —Proper face on him. And he laughs to one of the others. Then he says to me, —Yeah? Want some, new boy?

I feel his breath on my face. Focus on his blazer, a darkening sky. The finches fly off and are replaced by starlings, triangular wings, twisting and soaring, a swirling black cloud. A falcon swoops, stark, into the cloud. The cloud explodes. Remember to breathe. Think about starlings. Think.

People often overlook the starling. I think that's a shame. Just because they're common doesn't mean they aren't fascinating. What I like more than anything else is their sociability. This can sometimes be mistaken for aggression, but I reckon one goes with the other – you see people piling out of the Brown Cow on Friday evenings and you'll know what I mean.

A lot of ornithologists go for the rare find. They are only happy if they spot a red-flanked blue tit or a buff-bellied pipit, say. But to me that's missing the point. Why not enjoy what's all around? If you live in Weaste, like I do, you might as well pray for manna as go looking for a short-toed treecreeper or a paddyfield warbler. I prefer the dandelion to the orchid and I love starlings.

2

It's easy to dismiss them as just another medium sized dull bird. But actually they're not black, but iridescent with blues, purples, greens, and a sort of a metallic sheen to it – like when you see a puddle where engine oil has leaked into it. The most interesting thing about the starling for me is their ability to copy the sounds around them, including car alarms, mobile phones and even the woman over the road who comes out at teatime to screech at her kids, —Emma! Hayley! Yer chips are getting cold!

It's because they are able to adapt to their surroundings, that they have been so successful – so why should other ornithologists be so sniffy about that and favour birds that aren't as successful? It's just snobbery, if you ask me.

There were about eight or nine of them on my table this morning before school. I put out some of the stale bread ends from last week. I roughly cut them up and soaked them in water. You're not supposed to put dry bread out because it can swell up inside their stomachs and cause all kinds of problems. The tits and the finches made way for them and pretty soon the starlings were the only birds left.

There wasn't enough room for them all on my table so they took it in turns, queuing up along the washing line, flapping impatiently, sometimes squabbling about whose turn it was. I watched without thinking of the time. I made rough sketches of their activity, then looking over to the clock on the DVD recorder I noticed it was eight thirty. If I was to get to school on time I'd have to set off now, but I couldn't resist one last look at them as I grabbed my bag and my coat. I shouted up to mum, but she didn't hear me. Since she got with Tina, she doesn't get up in the morning any more to see me off. The door was on the latch, so I just had to close it gently behind me. I keep my key on a piece of string around my neck. I checked it was there before closing the door.

At the bus stop there were about five or six of my lot – Roseway School kids. They eyed me up but I pretended not to notice and stuck my head in my field guide. I knew they were

Roseway kids because they all wore navy blue blazers with the emblem, Roseway School: working together. I raised my head from my book and caught them eyeing me again. There was a girl of about fifteen and she nudged her friend and they giggled. I thought my zip might be undone but it wasn't. I could feel heat rising in my cheeks as I ducked behind my guide.

This is day three at my new school. There was a bloke at the bus stop with a baseball cap and four cans of Special Brew this morning. He had the small eyes and stooped gait of a cattle egret. He opened one of the cans and took a swig from it. He held one up for me but I shook my head. I rummaged for my sketchbook but when I found it I changed my mind and stuffed it back in my bag. I wanted to draw a quick sketch of him clinging to the beer can, but I was afraid he would ask me what I was doing. He stared at me so much that I was relieved when the school bus arrived.

I got on and paid my fare. I sat down at the front next to the luggage area, to make sure that no one could sit next to me. The bus was full of Roseway kids. Some of them would have made interesting studies but the bus was jolting too much for me to get my sketchbook out. They were noisy and played music through their mobile phones – mostly garage, bassline and niche sounds. I opened my book and pretended to read.

Day one, a Friday. Had the day off on Thursday, helping mum with the move. Arriving at the school I noticed the razor wire surrounding the fence, with a Care Bear garrotted by the razor wire. At the time, I'd wondered how long the bear had been there, but now, standing in this corridor, the ring leader's breath hot on my face, his spit on my cheek, I'm totting up how long *I've* got to do. Don't think about the ringleader, think about days, times, dates. Things you can count.

It's March, and school finishes in July. Four months. Four letters in June and July, five in March, but only three in May. Right now, I need to get through the next three minutes. Don't move. Don't speak. Don't look him in the eye. Navy blue sleeve.

Focus on those few months left and imagine they are a navy blue sleeve.

—This is Paul Cooper, the teacher said, holding me up like an item for auction, like those blokes with weird jackets on daytime TV. All the class seemed to be united in disapproval. They wouldn't be buying this lot number. — I'm sure you'll all make him feel welcome, he said. I could feel my cheeks going robin red. I looked at them all in rows staring back at me like the seabirds at Bempton cliffs, then I looked at my shoes.

The number three. Three posters on the wall. The third one is the school rules. Three rules. Rule number three: always have three bars of your tie showing at all times. Three letters in May, three days you've been here. Three days in and you still don't know where the classrooms are. Your timetable does not include a map although there is a plan of the building near the entrance of the school, which is why you are here now, trapped. You got lost and headed back to the main hall. You found the plan, worked out a route, then you got distracted by the display board, in particular Mr Hulmes's bushy eyebrows. Only got yourself to blame. When the bell went, it hardly even registered. There were others around but then you were on your own.

Nowhere to run. I'm worried I'll wet myself and they'll all see. He's up close now, the ringleader boy with the straw coloured hair like a black-necked grebe's face-tufts. He is shouting, bunched fists, he's about to whack me one, I tense, get ready. Then a boy appears from the other end of the corridor. He's taller and broader with short black hair. He seems to shimmer with the light behind him from the end of the corridor. He gives a quick look round, surveying the lie of the land. He smiles, the light making his outline silver, then he swanks across and the ring leader boy is backing off. The rest of the gang have flown.

The boy outlined with silver light is thinking how small the ringleader boy is. The ringleader boy shrinks in his presence,

5

like the silver light is pressing down on his lungs, squashing all the air out of his chest, making him small and dull.

And now the ringleader boy backs off some more. He sort of smiles at me in front of the silver swanking boy, like he's apologising. The swanking boy could split his head in two with his fist. He could bust his nose with the flick of his finger. Blood, an explosion of crimson liquid spraying out. The swanking boy could throw him across the room with one hand, he could smash him into the wall. The ringleader boy would crumple. He would make a noise like a tin of lager being prised open. The silver boy could get him on the floor with one push and kick him in the head. But the silver-black head of the boy does not move, his fist does not clench, his boot does not rise. He does not need to raise his hand, he does not need to raise a finger or an eyebrow. He just needs to stand there and the ringleader boy has gone. The corridor is empty apart from me and the shining silver boy.

—You new here? He asks me, as though just passing the time of day. I nod. My mouth has gone dry, so I don't risk speaking.

The boy just shrugs, like he couldn't care less. He struts off. I watch him leave. There is such confidence in his gait. Everything seems clearer, the colours of the posters along the corridors, brighter. I feel jittery and light headed, like I've just slugged a glass of whisky. I look over to where the ringleader boy was. He is lucky to have gone. He is lucky not to be on the floor in a puddle of his own thick blood. The girl who they were kicking has gone too. Drops of blood, a clump of hair on the floor of the corridor. The floor marked with signs, keep to the left, lines marking where to walk. I think about the redpoll again. Its bright red forehead. And the rosefinch, so much red around its face, breast and rump. There's the goldfinch too. Whoever called it the goldfinch, definitely wasn't looking at its face.

I find a bench to perch on in the cloakrooms. My legs have gone weak and my head is buzzing. I can feel the blood squirt through my veins. I feel it pulse behind my eyes. I lean back against the wall, hard and cold and solid. The school seems more substantial than the last one. It's made out of brick. The last school I was at was made out of plasterboard because it was built on a marsh. Great areas for bird life, are marshes. I can only guess at the devastation the building of the school must have caused. Warblers, gulls, coots, maybe even a bittern. No, of course not a bittern. Not in Salford. Bitterns are usually southerners, very shy and difficult ones at that.

Although the school was only thirty years old, the science labs had sunk so much that they were on the same level as the all-weather pitch. There were holes in the walls along the corridors where people had kicked them. This place is more like an open prison, with harsh lighting, bare brick walls, high fences and razor wire.

I open my book, A Field Guide to the Birds of Britain and Europe. The first page is missing because I had to tear it out. It had a library stamp. I took it from Salford library when I was ten. I've had to Sellotape some of the pages together. The Sellotape has darkened to the colour of vinegar. I like the way the book is organised. There's an introduction and a preface, then lots of background stuff on topography and even lists of ornithological societies. But the best bit is the checklist. Eight pages listing all the birds in order of nomenclature rather than alphabetically. I tried explaining this to my English teacher at the previous school but she didn't know what nomenclature meant and I got detention.

By each bird is a little box you can tick. I've managed to tick off 187 I've seen in the wild. Seeing them in sanctuaries doesn't count. There's a total of 636 birds, but a good number of these aren't native to Britain, nor are they visitors, so I reckon I've seen about half the birds on the list so I'm doing ok. As I look down the list, I see that I've not ticked the box next to sanderling. I take out my pencil and tick the box. I saw several sanderling last year along the Dee estuary, a small, plump, energetic little bird. So that's 188 birds. I write my score in the margin. As I do, I spot a bag stuffed under one of the benches. I'm about to open it when I see a teacher approaching. I shove it into my inside pocket.

—Shouldn't you be in class? What are you doing here?

Not a teacher of mine I don't think. I've managed to produce some saliva now, so I answer him, —Er, I'm new. I'm not sure where I'm supposed to be.

—Where's your timetable?

I put my book away and root for it in my bag. I hand it to him. He scrutinises it. —Double Maths, he says, —Mr Wilson, room number E14. It's this way, come on.

He waits for me to get up and then walks me to the room. All eyes are on me as he opens the door and we walk in. He says something to the teacher, this Mr Wilson, and Mr Wilson looks me up and down. I'm in luck because this teacher leaves and Mr Wilson escorts me to a spare seat, next to the swanking boy. He stares out of the window and doesn't acknowledge me. He just stares out of the window, his outline black and silver. I sit down and get out my book. His short black glossy hair coupled with his fearlessness, makes me think of a number of the corvids. So I look at this boy, and I wonder what bird he is.

The Collared Dove

I take a diversion on the way home and head for the precinct. I've spent double maths next to the swanking boy and normally double maths would be a struggle, but not today. I find the maths exercise books, with their square grid pages, really useful for sketching. In the space of an hour I manage to do a series of nine sketches. The first is a warm-up, and I do an egg. Drawing an egg is a good exercise to get things going. The top of the egg is a bit flat, but I'd need to turn my book round to get it right and I don't want to draw attention to myself.

On the second page I do a chick hatching out of the egg with its beak open. I think the teacher is doing quadratic equations. I don't take much notice but I realised a good while ago that if you want the teacher to ignore you, the best way is to keep your pen on the page and your head down. The third picture is the mother, or I suppose it could be the father, but I decide it's the mother, feeding a bluebottle to the chick. The mother looks like a starling so I draw on a few of the spear shaped chevrons that fleck their wings.

I turn the page and start on the fourth picture. Now the infant bird has adult wings and he perches on a post, with his wings stretched out, getting ready to fly for the first time. I do a little sun in the background. I turn the page again and sketch a sort of swirl, like a fluting shape, which is supposed to be the flock or swarm of starlings and then I do my starling flying to greet them. I look over to the boy to see if he has noticed, but he's just staring out of the window like a statue, a shimmering silver black statue. He's making it quite obvious he isn't working and I'm surprised the teacher doesn't say anything.

I turn over and do the next sketch. My starling has found a mate and I draw them breeding. For the seventh sketch I show my starling in the gutter, his toes curled up, his eyes eaten away – stone dead. I manage to finish the sequence before the bell goes with two quick sketches of his skeleton – the final one a close-up of his skull. Still the boy hasn't looked over to see what I'm doing, which is a shame because I think he'd like the skull.

I pop into the pet shop and buy a bag of sunflower hearts and some mealworms. I decide to take the long way back through Buile Hill Park. I pass Larder's café. I've just got enough left to buy a cup of tea. The woman gives me a little stainless steel teapot and I help myself to a cup and saucer and a jug of milk. It's busy and there aren't that many spare tables but I find one and sit down. There are two empty margarine tubs placed on the floor beneath a leak and there's a plop each time drops fall from the ceiling. I've been to this café before but not for a while. It's so blue and yellow, very much the colouring of a blue tit. Yellow lino floor with flecks of blue, yellow metal-framed benches with blue cushions stuck to the seats, blue glazed tiles and yellow grouting. Then, right in the middle of the café, a black old-fashioned lamp tapering up with two metal branches poking out at each side like burnt matchsticks. A teacher told us, when we went to Salford Museum at my last school, that they were for the lamplighters to prop their ladder against. Then there's a big white glass ball perched on top – a golf ball on top of a tee.

The funny thing is, someone has drawn a face on the ball with big jug ears and a smiley tooth-filled mouth, as if the person responsible realised that the lamp didn't look right and needed brightening up to match the surroundings. Except it doesn't brighten the place up, it makes it in some way darker, like the painted-on smile a clown wears, or the about-to-eat-you grin of a shark.

There's a chalkboard with some writing on: Afternoon Special Mon – Fri 2-4pm, pot of tea or regular coffee with a toasted fruit teacake £1.25p. Which explains why the place is so busy, mostly with old women gabbing.

I walk through the gates of Buile Hill Park from the Seedley end, up the hill to the middle. From the top of the park you can see all of Weaste and Seedley and the surrounding area. There are some kids on skateboards and a man with a beret on and a Weimaraner dog. You can see a grey concrete high-rise with red writing down its side: Salford Shopping City, it says, with a big red arrow pointing down. I don't know about 'Shopping City' though, there's just a T.J. Hughes, a Timpsons, a Wimpy, Home Bargains, a pet shop which also sells second-hand books, video cassettes, DVDs and CDs, three charity shops and Larder's café.

To the left of me is Weaste and to the right it's a bit posher. The trees in the park are well established, the buds about to burst. Green shoots on the grass, underneath are daffodils about to sprout. The houses on the right are big and the streets are leafy. It's like the park is a wall between two areas. I pass a white X painted onto the trunk of a tree, marking it out as dead so the man can chop it down.

The bowling green is surrounded by red brick walls painted with red paint over the top, as if the brick wasn't red enough. A jogger goes past with his chow, tail curled up and its dark purple tongue lolling. I notice a dog ball, one of those with a rope attached, dangling from a branch like a bauble hanging from a Christmas tree. Slate grey clouds, edges of white and yellow poking through.

I head for home down Weaste Lane and onto Gore Crescent. It's a better area than when we were here before, some poor bits but not like Ordsall with the trackies on one side and the suits on the other. Lots of red brick terraces, but more seem to be bought now than rented. They back on to each other so there are cobbled back-ins between them, with grey wheelie bins with pink lids outside the backyards, except some of the back-ins have been gated and locked with black metal bars, so that the wheelie bins have been left out in front of the gates, all jostling for room. Each has a number on, as though there's any difference between them.

These houses, the ones with the gated back-ins, have hardwood window frames and curtains and ornaments. Our street has white PVC window frames and To Let signs outside attached to the red brick walls. There are two collared doves rubber-necking by a Kenny yellow skip. Gore Crescent is long with lots of different houses. There's one with two pot sailors in the yard, blue and white, and one with a red and black flag flying with a picture of that bearded bloke you see on student T-shirts. I stop and have a look at it flapping in the breeze. Then I notice, standing beneath it, an old man with long white hair staring right at me.

I look away.

Babblers

I crossed over the road as I came down Gore Crescent to avoid a gang and saw a group of long-tailed tits in the willow trees outside number 55. About six of them. They're sociable like that. I like the mix of pink with black and white. Long tailed tits are not classed as true tits – they're known as babblers. Most true tits have black bibs, white cheeks and black or dark caps. In true tits the sexes are alike.

When I open the front door, which leads straight from the pavement to the living space, mum is on the sofa with Tina. She looks embarrassed, as though I've caught her doing something she shouldn't. She clasps at a green corduroy cushion.

—Ok? Mum says.

—Sorry I'm late, I say.

She looks at the clock on the DVD. It says, 16.35. I'm an hour late.

—I went to the precinct.

—What for?

I hold up my bag of sunflower hearts and mealworm.

—I've been trying to get hold of you, she says.

I take my phone out of my pocket. —It's gone blank, I say, holding it up. It's not been the same since I dropped it a few months ago.

Mum gets up and puts on her slippers. —How was it then?

I shrug.

—Well? she says, —What was it like?

I wonder why it has taken her three days to ask. —It's big, I say eventually.

She pulls her hair off her face. —You'll get used to it, she says. —You'll see. She smiles awkwardly. —And there's the trip.

I close the door and take off my blazer. It's hard to know where to put anything because there are boxes everywhere full of stuff. There are pictures that haven't been put up yet and loose bits of newspaper spilling from boxes where mum has had a look to make sure they are in the right room. There's a box of plates and mugs that should really be in the kitchen. I drape my blazer over the armchair. Mum's unpacked the mirror and placed it over the mantelpiece. She goes over and examines her face. She re-applies her lipstick. She wets her finger and preens her eyebrows. In birds you call the eyebrow the supercilium, which means, above the eyelash. The long-tailed tit has very striking supercilia – big black wedges arching right back. My mum's supercilia have been plucked to such an extent that there isn't that much there. She has to draw some of it back in with a pencil.

—We're going out, so you'll have to make you're own tea. Is that alright?

I nod. There's plenty in the freezer. Mum and Tina leave the room. My task for tonight is to sort out my three boxes of bird books, first tea then sort out the books. I'm hungry, so I pour myself a bowl of Frosties first, before tackling the freezer. Over by the window now, I shovel the sugary flakes and milk into my mouth, while watching the table.

At first there isn't much action. But then there's a robin. He hops onto the sunflower seed dispenser, rummages for one of the succulent hearts and flies off, mandibles wedged open with the seed. Shortly after, a pair of coal tits arrive. Nervy little birds, they twitch and jerk about. I pick up my binoculars to take a closer look. *He* could be a *she*. A female coal tit and a male coal tit are identical.

I put a lasagne in the oven and open the fridge. There are some of Tina's lagers, so I take one and open it. I didn't like lager at first, I was more of a cider drinker, or wine, like mum,

14

but I've developed a taste for it now. It's cold and crisp on my tongue. The lasagne is going to take about half an hour. The microwave was broken so we didn't even bother bringing it with us – we left it in the back car park with Heather's dresses and Heather's shoes and Heather's bags. I sit down at the table with my lager and my book. I take out a sketchpad and start to do some rudimentary sketches of tits.

I find it really hard to distinguish the marsh tit from the willow tit, and I find that by drawing them, identification becomes easier. The only real difference is that the bib of the marsh tit is slightly smaller than the bib of the willow, and also the willow has a light area on the edge of its wing feathers. In my sketches of the two birds I accentuate the differences and draw a big black line to the light wing edges and write WILLOW in capital letters. Then I draw another big black line to the bib of the other bird and write MARSH.

Once I've finished the sketches I close my book and take out another one of Tina's lagers from the fridge. I lever the ring-pull open and swig. I walk back through the living room and the unpacked boxes, and open the front door. I stand in the doorway with lager in one hand looking up and down the street. There are a few kids standing outside Kaz's shop, one is on a bike, and as a man passes, she asks him if he'll buy her some cigarettes. He doesn't even acknowledge her, just carries on walking.

Next to Kaz's is a Chinese called Golden Star, next to this is Zion Afro Store, then a Coral betting shop. There's quite a lot of activity. A couple walking hand in hand. He's got a brindle pit-bull with a thick leather harness. She wears white leggings and sucks the top off her ice cream. There's a big poster for Scorpion Lager outside the Gore Social Club at the end of the street. There's a group of smokers standing beneath it. It's a white drawing of a scorpion on a black background. This is a lager that can sting, drink me if you dare, it seems to be saying.

An old man walks past them wearing a navy blue cap with earflaps and carrying a canvas bag. He disappears into the betting shop, as a man in a black hoodie and a hi-vis waistcoat comes out, almost bumping into him. A dark skinned man in a grey baseball cap and a black beard posts leaflets through letterboxes. A kid with a staffy and a golf club. What are all these people doing? All the bald hard men with dogs, the old blokes with funny hats and doddery walks, the kids on bikes with hoods up, the old women wrapped in macs and clutching bags, the women with young clothes and young shoes and young hair, with old necks and old lips and old eyelids. They all seem to be going somewhere, or coming from somewhere.

I turn around and look up the other side of the street. There are a group of five, all about my age, walking down the road. Three boys and two girls. I wonder if they go to Roseway – I don't recognise them without their uniform. They seem full of energy and life, they laugh and nudge each other. The boys jostle and elbow and shove, the girls shriek and chatter. One of the girls is pretty, with long silky brown hair and tight jeans. As they pass by, the pretty one nudges one of the boys. They both look at me and snigger. I feel my cheeks flush and take a good swig from the lager. I look up to the sky, grey, darkening high cloud as far as the eye can see.

I'll sort out those boxes, I think, but then I remember, it's The Met on television and I never miss The Met. There's always something exciting going on, people getting shot, police chases, fast cars, drugs. It's never dull. My mum used to get worried about me, because I wanted that excitement. She was afraid I'd go to prison. But it's just a television programme.

Hornbills

The next morning I place bread crusts on the table and come back into the kitchen. I've also placed some bacon rind there. It would be nice to attract some corvids or even some raptors. In Ordsall, we had a sparrowhawk that was a regular visitor. I sometimes called into the butchers for scraps, but there isn't a butchers round these parts.

The starlings are there straight away, fighting over the bread. They gorge themselves in a frenzy. I make a quick head sketch to capture that quality a starling has, of being both human and reptilian. I can hear mum's headboard banging against the bedroom wall directly above me. I grab my bag – time to catch the bus. I go to the stairs.

I shout half-heartedly — I'll be late back Mum, school trip.

She doesn't hear me. But I've got my mobile so I can ring her later. Seems a strange thing to be doing, this trip. The coach sets off from school at nine, but it takes four hours to get to London, so we won't get there till one. That only leaves three hours to walk around the Tower of London, because the coach sets off back again at four, getting us home at eight. Seems a bit of a waste of time, but the school has received some funding for a history project, and our class was chosen. I've picked three books to take with me. My field guide, my sketchbook and a large hard-backed book on hornbills that I took from Manchester Central Library two years ago but still haven't had a chance to read.

I chose it primarily because I liked the picture on the cover of a black hornbill with a flame-red bill. You don't get hornbills in Salford, but it's good to learn about non-native birds. Birds, like anything else, are a product of their environment. There are 57 different species of hornbill, many of them endangered.

By the time I get to the school gates the coach is already loading. There are about thirty in my class and they are lined up ready as the teacher counts them off. I see the swanking boy from day three, who I now know is called Ashley, some way off in the distance. He is talking to a man in a car. He leans on the window of the driver's side of the car. The man inside is talking to Ashley but I can't hear what he is saying. The man's expression is stern. Ashley nods his head solemnly.

I make a quick sketch. The man passes Ashley a bag, which Ashley shoves into his inside coat pocket. The man points his finger at him. Ashley shrugs. The teacher has counted in all the class now. He sees me and looks down his list, slightly puzzled.

—Has anyone seen Tom Reed?

I don't hear anyone answer. I bag my sketchbook and walk over to the coach. Ashley appears and pushes in front. The teacher ticks me off his list.

—Come on, we need to go. But we're already inside.

In the coach I manage to get a seat near the front on my own. There's a bit of a commotion at the back where most people want to sit and some shoving and general jostling. Some of it is jokey and there's laughter but there's a bit of an edge too. They're sorting out a hierarchy I suppose, like birds do. One of the teachers chirps up.

—Hurst, sit down, stop messing about.

—It was him sir. He's got my seat.

—Just sit down there.

—But I was there first, swear down sir.

Things calm down a bit and the driver sets off. There's still a lot of joking and shouting.

—There's Reeko, eh Reeko!

Someone is banging on the window.

—Ugghhh.

18

—He's like shhhhh.

—What?

—What, no one puts it on the T-shirt?

—How do I spray myself?

—Do it underneath, shhhhh like that.

—What time is it bastard?

—See that car?

—Wow!

—Sick.

Lots of laughing. It's like I'm invisible. Perhaps I'm not really here. Then he appears. Ashley. He sits on his own in the middle of a double seat. I watch the girl in the seat next to him. She wants to sit next to him but there is no room. Ashley has taken all the room. She wants him to flirt with her. I should be sitting with a girl, I think. She is pretty and her breasts push open her blouse to reveal the edges of her white lace bra. Her skin is creamy and smooth. I imagine I'm sitting where she would like Ashley to be, sitting next to her. I needle her just below her rib cage with my finger and she giggles. Then she looks over to me and notices me staring at her. I bury my head in my book but make a sideways glance. She whispers something to her friend and points to me. Ashley watches her and laughs.

—Hey, what's your name? he shouts over to me.

—Cooper, I say.

I go back to my book. The girl nudges her friend again. I can feel their eyes on me, marking me out, separating me from the others. Ashley watches them nudge and whisper and he looks over to me and smiles. His black hair shimmers.

—What you reading? he shouts over.

I hold up my book and show him the cover.

—What you reading that for?

I shrug and go back to reading it, but I don't actually read the words, I just stare at their shape on the page.

—Eh! he shouts.

I ignore him and focus on the page more intently. Ashley walks over and sits next to me.

—Hey. I asked you a question, what's so interesting about that book?

He's very close to me now, almost touching. I show him the page I'm reading. There's a large colour photograph of an African ground hornbill.

—If this bird lands on your roof, you have to move house.

—That right? Ashley looks over to the girls, winks, but they have moved on to talk about something else. They are no longer staring at me.

—Why's that then?

—You have to move or else you die.

Ashley laughs and shakes his head. He grabs my sketchbook and starts to flick through it. He flicks past the sketches of mum at the kitchen table smoking a Regal, the marsh and willow tits with lines marking their differing bib sizes, the head of the starling, and it's too late as I realise what's on the next page. Ashley sees it, a sketch of himself, leaning against the car window, the space between the elbow and his torso forming a triangle, with a man pointing his finger in the middle of the triangle.

—What's this? he says.

I shrug.

—Eh? He points to the sketch of himself, puzzled and annoyed at the same time. He rips out the page and screws it up, puts it in his pocket and goes back to his seat. The girl with the breasts pushing out is muttering something to the other girl. They mutter and giggle as Ashley sits in the middle of his seat and stares out of the window.

But then he looks back at me, this time not annoyed, just puzzled. He takes out the crumpled paper and uncrumples it. He holds it up towards me like a flag and then points at it with his head. He makes a fist and pushes the paper down deep into the fist with his index finger. He holds the fist up, in the light, slowly it unravels. Five fingers, a palm. No paper. I go back to my book and give another sideways glance. I imagine reaching for the girl. I cup the back of her head with my hand and kiss her on the lips. She opens her mouth. I take my other hand and place it over one of her breasts. I squeeze it. My hand moulds the flesh and I feel the heat of her and her nipple stiffen under my palm. I feel myself getting hard and place the book on my lap so no one can see. I put my hand underneath and move my pants to make room for the growing feeling down there.

Hornbills are really fascinating. They are the only bird that has the first two neck vertebrae fused together – I imagine because of their enormous bills. There are loads of myths and superstitions about them. In Borneo, they believe that the birds transport the souls of the dead to God or to the devil. There's another tribe who believe that seeing the bird means a storm is brewing. Most of these superstitions, it has to be said, put the birds in a very bad light. It seems they get the blame for everything. They can't put a foot right.

We are split into two groups by a man with a loud voice and a moustache – he wears this bizarre outfit, red and dark blue with a picture of a red crown and a big E and an R underneath. He reminds me of the Queen's men in the cartoon Alice in Wonderland. And then just ordinary shoes – not old-world style. Regular black shoes you get at Timpson's – the sort my uncle would buy for one of the interviews that never result in a job but which he's encouraged to go to by the job centre. My uncle says they double as funeral shoes. The man with the loud voice and a moustache is talking to us. His movements are very stiff and his voice, very deliberate – I imagine he was a sergeant in the army.

Another man appears in the same ridiculous costume and he takes the first group, the one with Ashley in. I was standing close to Ashley thinking this would get me in the same group, but the man went, —one, two, one, two... Tapping us on the head and giving us each a number. I was a number two but for some reason he missed Ashley off the list and he has gone with the ones. The men in ridiculous costumes are called Yeoman Warders.

—Where are the ravens? I ask the man. He looks affronted, then addresses the crowd.

—This one's keen, he says, smiling at them all. Then he turns to me. —You'll get to see them when we go inside the grounds.

We are standing on a bridge, which goes over what was a wet moat but is now just grass. He's telling us the history of this and pulls his face when he talks about all the sewage it carried. The towers loom and there are wrought-iron gates and spikes. Some of the spikes were used to display human heads, like a trophy cabinet. We walk through one of the turrets, along a cobbled alley and go inside one of the towers.

There are various contraptions used for torturing people. There's one called a Scavenger's Daughter, which doesn't look that bad really. It's an A-frame metal rack. The head of the victim is strapped to the top bit of the A, the hands and legs at the lower bit. So you are in a sitting position. I can think of worse things, but the man makes a face again – and says it was excruciating. There's the rack, of course, but everyone's already seen this in films, although one of the girls makes a joke about Hayley Walsh needing it. Hayley Walsh is short and fat – the others laugh. Hayley looks away and pretends not to hear, but her eyes are filling up.

The man tells us about executions with particular relish. We go past Traitors' Gate. The water is a sage green colour and I like the lattice pattern of the wrought iron. Everything takes a long time, the crowd takes forever to get from one thing to another.

—This is known as the Bloody Tower.

Susan, the girl with the breasts pushing out of her blouse, says, —why's that then?

He's talking about two brothers now who were murdered. His eyes pop out and everyone laughs. I think about the ravens. I'm getting butterflies.

—Walter Raleigh, Guy Fawkes, Rudolf Hess were all here. Even the Krays, he says. —Have you all heard of them? Some nod, although not Hayley Walsh, she still seems upset about the rack joke. I watch Susan. I like the way her hips curve out and I wonder how smooth her flesh is between her legs.

I sit down and start sketching. I draw Susan with her legs open, with a sort of gateway at the end with a fine lattice pattern. The group move off again and I have to catch up with them. We meet up with the other party, but there's no Ashley. There are also no ravens, not that I can make out. There are quite a few crows, and I keep getting excited thinking they are ravens. And there are gulls. I like gulls, particularly their shrieking voices that echo. The teacher is looking around, concerned.

We are over by the chopping block near the white tower, which looks fantastic. Old bone.

—This is where Anne Boleyn was beheaded, he tells us. She wasn't beheaded with the axe he is holding, but with a sword. It's great here. The grass is really green, and I wonder whether it's because of all the blood that's seeped through the soil. It probably makes good fertilizer, lots of iron and other nutrients. The Yeoman Warder tells us one of the last things Anne Boleyn said to the constable of the tower was, —I hear the executioner is very good and I have a little neck. He makes his voice go high when he says this. Everyone laughs.

I imagine her bent over the chopping block, but apparently she sat upright. The swordsman cut her head off with a single swipe. Still no ravens. I keep thinking I've seen them, only for them to be crows. I ask the Yeoman Warder again. He tells me there's a Ravenmaster whose job it is to look after them. I'll be able to spot him, he says, because he has a little raven sewn into his sleeve. Then he pats me on the shoulder, a bit too hard for it to be friendly.

23

I spot Ashley by the wall in the opposite direction. He is looking over the other side. And then I see it, perched on the rim of a bin, stooped over, hunched, a huge cloak the colour of oil, its beak like the head of a pickaxe. It's a raven. This close up, there's no mistaking it for a crow. It seems to be about three times the size and its beak is huge, its plumage slicker, more iridescent. It looks wonderful and I get a chill right down my back. It sticks its head in the bin and pulls out a half-eaten sandwich. I stare in wonder at its beauty.

—That's a big crow, Susan says.

—It's a raven, I say. —They live here.

—How do you know that?

—If the ravens leave the tower, Britain will disappear into the ocean.

—Bollocks! says Ashley, as he walks up behind me. He clips me round the ear and smiles. Susan doesn't pay him any attention. She seems to be interested in what I am saying.

—It was a raven that showed Cain where to bury Abel.

She doesn't seem impressed. —Why don't they just fly off?

—Their wings. They've been clipped.

I've lost her, she's walking off. Ashley follows, mock-skipping. He pretends to grab her arse, then winks at me. I watch her skirt rise and fall. I watch her calf muscles tense and relax. In my mind I put my hand on her bum and she lets me leave it there.

I spot a Warder with a raven sewn into his sleeve and I ask him if he is the Ravenmaster. I get talking to him. He feeds them on beef he gets fresh every day from Smithfield Meat Market. He tells me there are eight ravens and he tells me all their names. He says there were nine but Grog, the ninth, went AWOL and was last seen outside an East End pub.

—That one's Thor, he says, and he's sixteen.

Same age as me. But the oldest raven ever was called Jim Crow and he lived to 44.

We go into the White Tower. The Warder tells us it was built in 1078 by William the Conqueror. There are hundreds of swords and axes and cannons and every kind of weapon on display. We've only got a bit of time left though, the teacher says, and he tells us to meet him by Tower Green in an hour. I decide to make my way to the gift shop.

There's all kinds of tat in there. Plastic luminous ghosts with a ball and chain around them, plastic skeletons wielding swords, Yeoman figurines made out of cheap plaster, a Beefeater pencil, a Union Jack tie, a Tower of London visor, heraldic spoons, a cannonball key ring, but there's a sizable book section and I rifle through it. Lots of books on the history of the tower, even a book on Jack the Ripper. Then I find it, a hardback book with a picture of the king of the crows on the front: The Raven, by Derek Ratcliffe. I open it and read the first paragraph:

> The place of the raven in myth, legend and history is long established, and this book describes the bird's fall from grace as a valued scavenger in medieval cities to a persecuted outcast in the modern wilds...

There are chapters on every aspect of the bird, even maps at the back with breeding sites indicated. I feel a hand on my shoulder. It's Ashley. He picks up a souvenir guardsman pen and pockets it. He takes a policeman's helmet pencil sharpener and nabs that too. He looks around for other things to steal.

—You getting that? he says, pointing to the book.

—No money, I say.

He just shrugs. Then he gives me a nudge. He picks up the book and has a quick look round. The two women behind the counter are talking to each other and not looking at us. I open up the top of my bag and he slides it in. He taps me on the back. It feels good – like we're a team. He leans into me.

—Now you do me a favour.

He leads me out of the shop and towards the wall I saw him leaning over earlier on. He doesn't seem to be able to find what he's looking for.

—What is it?

—Never mind, just keep a look out.

He leans over the wall again. I see a black car move across the car park with tinted windows and Ashley watches it too, its slow approach. It pulls up as close to the wall as it can get. A man gets out and walks across so that he is directly underneath Ashley. He gives Ashley the nod. Ashley takes out the bag from his inside pocket I saw him put there this morning and he hovers it over the man. The man holds out his hands ready to catch the bag. Ashley is about to drop it and the man uses hand signals to urge him on, but then he smiles back in defiance at the man.

Anger flashes across the man's face. Ashley teases the man with the bag, pretending to drop it and then dangling it again. The man points to Ashley and draws his index finger across his neck. He points again and mouths 'You're dead'. Ashley sticks two fingers up at the man. I spot the teacher walking over and I warn Ashley. He sees him just in time and stuffs the bag back inside his pocket.

—What are you doing? the teacher says.

—Just enjoying the scenery, Sir.

We join the rest of the group at Tower Green.

—Why did you do that?

Ashley looks at me and smiles, —Cos I've had an idea.

Rooks

I keep having this dream where I'm caught in quicksand but am always rescued at the last minute. Sometimes, in the dream, I'm genuinely scared for my life, but other times it's humiliation that's the main feeling. It's similar to a dream I used to have when I was still in primary school, where I would fall into shit. Sometimes it was a sewer, or a latrine and I thought I was going to drown. Often there would be a pretty girl close by I was eager to impress, or sometimes a boy I was keen to get in with. I don't really think dreams mean anything.

But I do have one dream over and over that is actually real. I dream I can fly and the thing is, I think I have flown before. No, I don't think, I know. I have flown. It's quite hard to do and you need to concentrate a lot, but in the end you just reach up and as long as you have the balls to stick with it, then up you go. It's only when you bottle it, that's when you come crashing down. For years I believed I was the only one who could fly but now I think I've found someone else. Something about his stance and the distance there is between us and the others. Also, his eyes. He has that same look in his eyes birds have. A bird is never in any doubt about its purpose. I think this person knows I can fly. He's recognised in me what I've recognised in him.

I do dream a lot about birds, and I suppose that's because I think a lot about birds. Particularly the rook. It is often mistaken for the crow, but is really quite different. It is slightly smaller and has a patch of bare grey-white skin around its bill. The voice is similar to the crow but sometimes a rook can sound almost human. There's a big rookery in the cemetery just up the road. They are a noisy bird and tend to wake me up quite early in the morning. They jag and clatter, like spilling the cutlery drawer on to the floor. You'd expect this harsh sound to annoy but in a strange way it soothes. It's the sound of the earth.

The cemetery is just one of a number of improvements on Ordsall. I saw a mosher this morning with a black hooded top, black baggy jeans and those spiky rubber rucksacks moshers have, and I saw that as a good sign. You don't get any moshers in Ordsall because it would be too risky. Occasionally, you'd get a mosher moving in, but within weeks, sometimes days, they'd have changed their hair and clothes to fit in. It never really felt safe to go anywhere in Ordsall.

I'd go to the general store opposite Salford Lads' Club now and again but only if it was light and if I saw a gang of boys I'd bolt back. There was a long street with red brick terraces but a lot of them were boarded up and it was a no man's land walking down that street. You'd be almost at the shop, then you'd see five or six kids, maybe one on a bike, a dog roaming loose, a white, a grey, a checked hooded top, chewing gum, blowing bubbles and popping them – bang, bang, bang, like a gun going off, and I'd just turn round and speed back.

The thing about Weaste, there's more open space, you don't feel hemmed in and cars and old people come past. The Metrolink slices right through it, two lines cutting Weaste in half and creating lots of space. Above the tramlines, tram wires go all the way down Eccles New Road.

When we lived in Broughton there was an area where all the Haredi Jews lived. You'd see them, father and son, son with long curly sideburns and a black bowler hat, dad in a black skirt with tassels either side, white tights, black shoes and a black coat. Or sometimes they'd have a white shawl with three black stripes along it, then on his head, well, they wear these funny hats that make them look like they are balancing a big black furry hatbox on top. Must take some guts that, but very few of the gang members would start trouble with them, not even the runners on BMXs. Even so, the Haredi Jews applied to the council for permission to have a wire around their area. A wire to keep out evil spirits. The council turned them down. My mum said they should have asked for razor wire not spiritual wire.

People say Broughton's rough, but I liked it. There are some nice old buildings and at the top, the cliff – great for birds. I never felt that threatened walking around Broughton, I always thought that if the Jews could get away with it, so could I. To them, I was probably just another scally. It amused me to think of it like that.

You never got drivers in Ordsall. You can't drive around the estate because of all the blue metal barriers and bollards and big boulders set in concrete. I could see why the council had done it, to stop the joy-riders, but it also stopped the police from patrolling, so it became a police-free zone. Walkways connected up the drives, groves, crescents and avenues – narrow walkways that penned you in. We lived in Nine Acre Court, a high-rise on the edge of the park. You could see Salford Quays from our front window. The Lowry Centre, hotels and museums, shopping and eating places. It was only walking distance but we never went there, just getting to the general store over the road from Salford Lads' Club was enough of a journey.

But in Weaste it feels different. Cemeteries are very good places to find birds and I'm delighted that Weaste Cemetery is so big and leafy. Thousands of gravestones, hundreds of trees and hundreds of birds. Why are cemeteries such good places for birds? I think because there are lots of worms. Why are there lots of worms? The reason there are lots of worms in cemeteries is because there is a lot of worm food. As the wooden caskets rot and split, the earth enters and with it, the worms.

Starlings, rooks, and crows seem to particularly enjoy gorging on the flesh of worms. There are so many worms in the rich soil, it's just a case of dipping your beak in. The worms feed on the decaying bodies of people and they become fat and sluggish, making it easy for the birds to feast on them. If you're a sparrowhawk it's a good place to hang out too.

I walked through the rows and rows of gravestones: in loving memory of Samuel Davies, Isaac Witter, Maude Speck, Phoebe Schofield, Sarah Slack, George Arthur Yardley, Charles Cooper... Could be a relative of mine, I thought. How ordered it all was. Good to see in death there is order. I thought about my own tombstone, I'd just like a big black stone with a skull and crossbones on and then underneath: Paul Cooper is dead. His rotting body lies beneath this stone and is being feasted on by worms, which in turn will be eaten by blackbirds and magpies – just the way it should be.

I've got a box full of bird skulls under my bed. The rook is one of my particular favourites. It's a shame that the skulls of tits and finches are too delicate to preserve. I've tried it a few times, but they tend to turn to dust. I tried putting them in matchboxes and wrapping cling-film around them, but give it a year or two and they generally crumble. The first tit skull I got was quite lucky. I was watching some blue tits on the nuts, when a magpie flew down and, like a pair of scissors, snipped off the head of one of the tits. The tit just stayed clinging to the nut bag, without its head.

I got some maggots, put them in a plastic tub with the head, and put a lid on it. With bigger skulls you can bleach them, but not with a tit skull. It took ages for the bugs to pick it clean, but it just turned to dust within a few weeks. Nothing smaller than a starling – that's my rule now. I used the headless body of the tit to entice raptors. I impaled it on a nail I knocked into the table.

The door opens as I'm pressing the blue-tacked corners of a sketch down.

—I'm going out, she says.

She is dressed up with lots of make-up on. She looks around at the room, noticing the changes. —Are you settling in then?

I nod and she smiles at me.

She looks around the room again and then says, —Are you alright Paul?

—Yeah.

—I mean, you're not in any trouble?

—Not this time mum.

—And school's ok is it?

—Yeah.

She lingers on the threshold clutching the door handle.

—It's better than the old school.

—Is it?

—It's made out of brick.

—That's nice, she says. She messes with the door handle, making it click.

—I hate to do this to you, you do know that?

I nod, but I don't really know what she's talking about. I'm getting concerned about the door handle now. What if it snaps off? I won't be able to close the door.

—It's just, sometimes you have to move... You'll understand when you're older. Things happen and... She starts to fidget with the door again. Click, click, click. —Then you have to go.

—It's alright mum.

Stop messing with the handle, I want to say. Get off the handle.

—I do think about you.

Click. Click. Click.

—I know... I know you do.

Take your hand off that handle. Before it breaks.

Click. Click. Click.

—And everything's ok?

No, everything's not ok. You are going to break the handle. Why does she do that? Why does she keep asking the same question? Does she think if she asks it enough I'll give a different answer? Perhaps if I give her a different answer she'll stop asking and get off the handle.

—I've got a friend.

—A friend?

—Yeah.

Her eyes light up. —Really? That's great. Who is he? Is it a he?

—He's called Ashley.

—That's a nice name. What's he like?

—I've not decided yet mum. I think he's one of the corvids.

Her look changes. She doesn't like me talking about birds.

—Well, I'm glad you've found a friend, Paul. Invite him round, he can stay over if he likes. I'd really like to meet him.

Is it a raven that Ashley most reminds me of or just a carrion crow? Mum lingers again and fiddles with the door handle. Then the beep-beep of the taxi outside.

—Look, I've got to go. You'll be ok on your own won't you?

—You go and have a good time.

Her and Tina go out most nights. It was the same with Heather, for the first six months. Then they used to sit on the sofa together drinking wine and watching soaps. Then Heather started going out by herself. We used to have nights in together then, which was nice. But sometimes mum would get upset and start to cry.

I can hear Tina stomping around downstairs. She will no doubt be looking for her keys or her phone. She always seems to lose them as soon as she puts them down.

—We won't be late, she says and I nod again.

Mum leaves the room when the taxi beeps again. I hear them walk to the door and the sound of the door as they close it. I check the door handle to make sure it's ok. Luckily the door still closes. I go downstairs and open the freezer. There's a pizza. I put the oven on and get one of Tina's lagers. It will only take about fifteen minutes for the pizza to cook. I take the can with me back to my bedroom. Only one box to sort out now.

Rummaging through the box, I come across some old photographs. One of me aged about three. I'm standing on the beach with mum and my sister, so it must have been my dad that took it. I'm holding an ice cream. I think it was Southport beach because there is no sea, just a lot of sand, like a desert.

There are no pictures of me as a baby, although there are hundreds of my sister as a baby, all more or less the same picture over and over again. Claire lying on her back in a stripy pink and white sleepsuit looking into the camera, Claire lying on her back in a stripy pink and white sleepsuit looking away from the camera. There are probably about thirty variations of this. There's also a whole sequence of Claire in a pram wearing matching red hat and mittens, and another sequence of near-identical pictures of Claire in a high chair wearing a towelling bib with a rabbit on the front. If you put them altogether and flick through them like a flicker book, it creates the impression that Claire is moving and breathing. I've often wondered why there are so many pictures of Claire and none of me.

I sort through some more until I come across the photograph I was looking for. Me with my dad. He's holding a raven, in mock-horror, a stuffed raven. I'm holding my dad's hand and my dad is holding the bird so it looks as though it is swooping down to get us. I think we were on holiday. It looks like the inside of an antique shop. There are other stuffed animals in the background, a badger, a fox, a pheasant, and some old furniture. I know this photograph very well, visiting the Tower of London yesterday reminded me of it. There's a message on the back, but I know what it says and I don't want to read it. In fact, I make a point of not reading it. This is the first photograph of me, aged three. It must have been the last holiday we had as a family.

Where to put the photograph? I pick up my bag and take out the book on ravens. I open it and flick through a few pages. I skim the writing until I find an appropriate passage:

> *The raven is a striking creature, largest of all the crow tribe, with a heavy pick-axe bill. In the rugged Lakeland fells it is largely a matter of searching the obvious crags one by one until all the nesting places are found. You will be glad to hear the croak of the raven that tells you, you are not alone...*

I place the photograph underneath and close the book.

I think back to a warm August afternoon. I've not started school yet but I know school is something that is going to happen to me soon. In my mind it seems exotic. Full of new people, new things, a new world. I'm in the park in the centre of the estate. Our house overlooks it. Nearly at the top of the climbing frame. My sister is on the swings. She's four years older. She's with a friend from school.

I don't like my sister but I'm happy and it doesn't matter. The climbing frame is lime green and acid yellow and candy floss pink and sky blue. And I'm trying to imagine what my first day of school will be like. You go there to learn things. What do you learn? My sister has homework. She has to wear a uniform. I don't like the sound of that. But she is always full of chatter, about her friends. What they said. What they did. We have a cat called Wolf and it is sitting on the bench watching us and watching some birds in the tree. Wherever we are the cat is usually close by.

I get to the top of the climbing frame, higher than anything else or anyone else in the park, on the same level as my bedroom. I look down at my sister. It feels good to tower over her. In my own mind I'm a giant. And walking through the estate people run away from me in fear. I look over to my house again. King of the castle. I can see my dad at the front window. My dad is watching me. It feels good to have a witness. I'm happy that my dad has seen me at the top of the climbing frame. It's the first time I've done it. For a moment I'm scared. Will I get told off? But no one told me I couldn't climb to the top. It's my sister who will get told off, because my mum told her to look after me.

My sister is ignoring me. That's fine by me. She shows off in front of her friends and makes jokes, about me. They are playing hopscotch. I can't see the point of hopscotch. I look at my dad again. My dad is still watching me. I wave at my dad and my dad waves back. I am happy. It is later, when I get home, that I find out my dad wasn't waving hello.

Now it is raining. We're watching television. Me, my sister and my mum. The rain is beating at the window. And my dad is at the window. My dad is knocking at the window. I look at my dad. My dad is pleading with me. Pointing to the door and mouthing words I can't hear. His hair is plastered to his face and water drips from it. My sister doesn't look at my dad. She stares at the television. My mum tells me to stop looking at my dad. Watch the television. She turns up the volume. But I defy her and look at my dad again. My mum screams at me. Watch the television. I do as I'm told. The knocking goes on for some time. Eventually it stops.

My dad has gone.

Black-Headed Gulls

I'm standing away from the crowd towards the all-weather pitch. You get a good view of the gulls from here. Most of the gulls you see in Salford are black-headed gulls. In fact, for some of the year a black-headed gull has a white head. There was a boy at my last school who was called Blackhead, but he didn't have a black head, his hair was more the colour of soot, which is dark grey rather than true black. Although a sea bird, the black-headed gull is not really found by the coast any more, where herring gulls and other large gulls tend to dominate. No, the black-headed gull has made our inland cities its home. Salford is ideal for black-headed gulls because of all the concrete high-rise buildings. To a black-headed gull the side of a council flat must seem like an improvement to the side of a cliff. Gulls are essentially scavengers.

One thing that really irritates me is people who say 'seagulls'. I've got tired of the amount of times I've had to explain to people there are no such things as seagulls. There are black-headed gulls and herring gulls, lesser-black-backed gulls, common gulls, little gulls, laughing gulls, great black-headed gulls, slender-billed gulls, ring-billed gulls, ivory gulls, kittiwakes... But no seagulls. There never has been and there never will be a seagull.

I notice Ashley standing near to a group of girls. He watches them and then looks over to me. He looks at them again and then at me. Then he shrugs. What do you think? He seems to be saying. The girls are lovely; there are some really developed ones who seem to burst out of their blouses. We both watch as they chatter together, teasing each other. One of them laughs and holds up her hands in mock-surrender. Ashley looks over to me. I let him know I'm staring at him this time. Why not? He holds my gaze for a few moments, then looks away. But in that gaze he has admitted he has found me, he has sought me out through the crowd. He must have received a text because he takes out his phone and reads it. He looks at it warily but tries not to show concern in front of the girls. He walks over to me.

—Here, come with me.

—What for?

—You'll see, he says, and leads the way.

We walk across the all-weather pitch, looking round to make sure no teacher is watching.

—Yesterday, you saw me give a bag to that bloke in that car, right?

He seems agitated. —What's the matter? I say.

—Never mind that, you just back me up.

I nod and we carry on walking. —Where are we going? I say.

—He's called Dave. Don't say anything unless he asks you, right?

We make our way over to the fence. Ashley is looking around nervously, making sure no one has seen us. We're not supposed to cross the all-weather pitch. A red car approaches, it pulls up close to the fence. Ashley gives me a stern nod, as if to say, get ready, or something like that. A man gets out of the driver's side.

—That's him, Ashley says. —That's Dave.

Another bloke gets out of the passenger side, who looks a bit like Dave. He has the same small pale eyes and thin lips, although he is younger, not as stocky. They walk over to us. They don't seem happy. They both look as though they could pull arms off babies and not give it a second thought.

—You sorted? Dave says to Ashley.

—Job done, Ashley says.

—Where's my money?

—Didn't get it, Ashley says.

—What you talking about? His eyes look kind of mad.

—I had to drop it from the tower, Ashley says. —I couldn't get to him.

—Is that right? Dave doesn't look like he believes Ashley.

—Yeah. He saw me.

He points to me, nudges me. I nod.

—What did you see? Dave asks me.

—He gave it to him. I say.

Dave weighs us both up. The other bloke just stands behind him staring at us.

—Come here, both of you. He leads us to where there is a gap in the fence and we crawl through it. The two men walk in front, we walk behind. Ashley turns to me with an expression on his face I have never seen before. Scared. He takes out a bundle from inside his jacket and hands it to me. It's very heavy but I don't have time to ask what it is. I hide it before the two men see us.

Twenty minutes later I'm standing outside a slate-grey shed at the back of an abandoned industrial estate. I pace around, not really knowing what to do. There are tufts of yellowing grass growing from the base of the shed. Coke cans and crisp packets are scattered everywhere. There's a half-empty bottle of Fanta and a dirty nappy. There's an off-cut of razor wire lying coiled like a snake nearby. I peer through the window and I see Ashley. He is strapped to a chair with gaffer tape wrapped tightly around his mouth, and the other bloke, who I have now learned is Dave's brother Andy, is holding a pair of long-nose pliers. The pliers remind me of the bill of a great snipe or perhaps a woodcock – long and sleek and straight. I don't know what to do. I look away. I try thinking about snipes. Snipes. What do I know about snipes? Not that much really. They are easy to spot by their zigzag flight and their hoarse rasping cry. They live in marshes, water-meadows, sewage farms, boggy moors – places like that.

It's my job to keep a look out or else. Or else what? I should have asked, or maybe not. I look in the window again. Dave is talking to Ashley. Andy takes Ashley's little finger and he pulls off the nail with the pliers. Ashley's eyes are bulging. Snot bubbles from his nostrils. I can see the veins in his neck protrude. Blood drips from his finger. I look away. Gulls fly past, shrieking. They seem to be saying, 'Claire, Claire, Claire...' Claire is my sister's name. I try and think of birds, but I can't think of anything.

Fears. I think about my fears. What am I afraid of? I am afraid of blood tests, people with small eyes, masks, my mum's older brother Tony, finding hair in food, my sister's ornamental dolls, being in the spotlight, swimming in water which isn't completely clear, tinned tuna, beetroot, ventriloquists' dummies, being sent to prison, being kicked out of home, storks, being trapped in a tunnel in a cave 1000 feet beneath the ground, being trapped in a lift, gangs of men who seem to be having a laugh but could easily tip over at any point, girls, the police, falling into a pit full of ravenous rats, losing my mum, eventually meeting up with dad only to find that he doesn't like me, going blind, being caught by my mum masturbating, being caught by my sister masturbating, being caught by Tina masturbating... I have an idea. I turn back to the window. Andy holds Ashley's finger. He is about to pull off another fingernail. I bang on the window, Andy and Dave turn to me, and I mouth the word: 'police'. They look to each other, Dave gives Andy a nod and then they run off. I watch them leave the scene. I hear them start their car and drive off. I go round the front of the shed and go inside. I unwind the gaffer tape from around Ashley's face. He gasps with relief. He gives me a look of gratitude. I start to untie his hands. There are red track marks where the twine has scorched his skin. Some of his skin has broken and there are traces of blood speckling the track marks.

We don't go back to school. Instead we find some wasteland on the estate where Dave won't be able to find us. We sit on a half-demolished wall. Ashley has his shoe off and is bandaging his bleeding hand with his sock. He finishes the job and puts his shoe back on, but the white sock is already turning red with his blood. Ashley's phone bleeps as he receives a text. He takes it out of his pocket. It's from Dave: *we avnt finished with u*. Ashley sort of shrugs this off and puts his phone back in his pocket.

—Let's go back to school, I say.

—What for?

I'm thinking that at least we'll be safe there. It's the one place Dave can't get us. But Ashley shrugs again. I look around. There are rooks circling above us. I watch their widening gyre as they rise on the thermals. I see Dave's red car pull up and I grab Ashley and we duck down behind the wall. We wait for the car to drive on and then we run in the opposite direction. We run until we reach a bit of scrubland with some trees and bushes. We sit on an upturned supermarket trolley and get our breath back.

—What we going to do?

—I'm thinking, Ashley says.

I watch him and wait for an answer, but there's no response. I try again.

—We can't go back there.

—No kidding, he says.

The full weight of the trouble we are in begins to press itself on top of me.

—Why don't you give the bag to Dave? I say.

—Cos I've already sold half of it, he says.

—What d'you do that for?

We both sit in silence for a while. I look around. There's an abandoned tyre covered in moss. Then I have an idea.

—We could go up to the Lakes.

—Where's that?

—Cumbria.

—Where?

I take out my book on ravens and hand it over to Ashley. He flicks through it.

—I've been reading this, I say.

—What is it? He flicks through it some more. —This the book you nicked?

—Yeah.

Ashley throws it back at me. I catch it.

—Crap, he says.

The nearest place from Salford where ravens breed in any significant number is Cumbria. They're the only corvids native to Britain that I've not seen in the wild. There's a nest in Helvellyn that's been there over fifty years. This is a good time of year too – mating season.

I'm thinking back to the Tower of London and that thrill, a wave travelling through my body. Ravens, so black and shiny and beautiful.

—It will be a laugh, I say, trying to convince Ashley.

—Nah.

—Well, what then?

—Come on, he says, and gets up.

I follow him. We walk through a sort of wood. Bluebell stems like maggots inch their way out of the earth. The first signs of spring.

—What is it you've got anyway?

He doesn't answer me at first, but then he stops and says, —You mean what *you've* got.

Then I remember the bundle. I reach in and feel.

—What is it?

—A few hundred Es, some skunk, a blotter sheet of acid, some coke and some ketamine, he says.

I've heard of these things from The Met, but I've never tried them or even seen them before. I know that they must add up to a lot of money though, just off Dave's reaction. Ashley takes the bag. He opens a packet of Regal and offers me one. I don't

41

really smoke, I've had a few of my mum's though, and it seems impolite to refuse. He lights it for me, he lights his own.

—So what we gonna do? I say.

—Have a look. And he nods at my coat again. I reach in once more and pull out a dull black metal shaft and a brown wooden handle. It's a revolver.

—Fuck. What have you got that for?

Ashley takes the gun and aims at me. —To shoot the fucker, he says.

I don't think we'll be going back to school today.

Shrikes

We walk through the streets of Weaste. Dodd Street, Peveril Road, along Gore Avenue, past the black barred gates across cobbled back-ins, between the red brick terraced houses, up through Seedley. We jump over the railings on Fitzwarren Street, past the mini-roundabout. We make our way through the market, heaving with punters and stallholders, onto the precinct, past a boarded-up pound shop and a Cash Converters store. We pass the post office with heaps of withered flowers outside from the latest joyride gone wrong.

The rain has soaked the condolence cards and you can't read what they say any more. There's a pie shop next door, they've had a delivery of mince which has spilled out of the van – there's a crow picking meat off the road. I watch it hop and strut, and then grab the mince in its beak, gobbling it down like it was a worm.

The sun beats down, the first heat of spring. It bakes the tarmac. A few scabby pigeons wait on the sidelines for the crow to finish its meal. A pigeon is good bait for a sparrowhawk.

—Shit, Ashley says.

I look to where he is looking. It's Dave's red car. Dave has seen us but his car is the wrong side of the dual carriageway. Dave mounts the island. He gets out and runs towards us, followed by his brother, Andy. We look around in panic. There's a man standing by the cash machine. His car is close by. We both run towards his car. Ashley jumps in the driver's side and I jump in the passenger side. The man sees us and runs across.

—Oi! he shouts, and starts to bang on the window, but Ashley quickly presses the central locking. The man is screaming at us now. Ashley starts the car and drives towards Dave. He swerves to hit him but Dave jumps out of the way. Andy, his brother, is in the middle of the road. Ashley smashes the car into him. There is a dull thud and Andy is flung into the air. I look back at Andy's crumpled body in the gutter by the spilt mince, as Ashley speeds off. Dave runs over to his brother, kneels over him. I see him feel for his pulse. There is blood everywhere. Dave puts his head in his hands.

We are at the junction waiting to turn left. I watch Dave still huddled over his brother. Then he looks up and sees me watching him. He gets up and starts to run at us. Ashley turns left and speeds off. I see Dave run over to his car and jump in.

My heart is thumping now. I try and find some music on the radio with the same beat. No sign of Dave. I find some banging house and look over to Ashley. He nods his head to the music and smiles to himself. He turns the volume up. I shout over it, —Do you think we've lost him? Ashley nods.

—What do you think happened back there? I say. Ashley shrugs. —With Dave's brother? I add.

—He'll be alright, Ashley says.

I look at Ashley but don't say anything. We drive in silence. I watch the bonnet of the car hoover up chevrons. It seems to do this in time to the thumping of the music and the effect is hypnotic, like watching a waterfall's foam cascading over a precipice. You focus on the whole and it seems to go fast, then you focus on one part and it slows.

And then I see it, and I can't quite believe it, but its outline is unmistakable and its markings leave me with no doubt at all – it's a red-backed shrike. A red-backed shrike perched on a fence post by the side of the road. I gasp with delight. A red-backed shrike. A bit bigger than a house sparrow, but slimmer. It's a male with a bluish-grey head and black bandit eye mask – like Zorro. A bright chestnut back and that bill – a really big hooked bill – more like a hawk's bill really. It's almost like a sparrow that's discovered meat, and is in the process of evolving from

44

one type of bird to another. It's wonderful. I want to tell Ashley, but fear he will spoil the moment.

I take out my field guide and scan the list. I find it and tick it off. That's 189 birds now. This is incredible, the red-backed shrike is virtually extinct in this country, you only really have a chance of seeing it in May or June as it migrates north, or August or September when it migrates south. A red-backed shrike in Salford in March – unheard of. I can only really put this good luck down to meeting Ashley. I can hardly contain my excitement.

—Fuck, Ashley says and, for a split second, I think it's his reaction to the red-backed shrike, but then I look in the rear view mirror. Dave is behind and gaining on us. Ashley puts his foot down and creates distance between us. We approach a crossroads. The lights are on red. He skips the lights, Dave follows, swerving to avoid an oncoming car. The car beeps long and hard.

There are cars in front of us that Ashley tries his best to overtake. He nudges between them but there isn't enough space. Dave is only a few yards away now. And then, crunch. Dave hits the back bumper. We both lurch forward. My field guide drops to the floor.

—Bollocks, Ashley says. He reaches into his coat and pulls out the revolver.

—Here, cop for this.

I look at the gun, not sure what to do.

—Shoot the fucker, he says, and throws the gun on my lap.

I look down at it. It feels heavy wedged between my legs. Ashley presses a button in his door and my window slides open. There is a dramatic gust of wind.

—Go on, he says.

I take hold of the gun and lean out of the window. I am smacked by a rush of air, I have to gasp to get my breath and my eyes water. I aim the gun at Dave, but I can't press the trigger. Something invisible is stopping me.

—Shoot! Ashley shrieks.

There's another crunch as Dave hits the back bumper again and I nearly drop the gun out of the car.

—Do it!

I lean out of the window some more, take aim but can't bring myself to fire it. Instead, I launch it at Dave's windscreen. It tumbles through the air like a boomerang then smashes into the glass, turning the glass into a sheet of white frost. Dave's car veers to the left, mounts the verge and crashes into a lamp post.

—What you do that for? Do you know how much that cost?

Ashley seems shocked to have lost his gun, but then, looking out of the rear window and seeing the smashed up car, his face changes. He laughs and I join in, more out of relief than anything else. Ashley whacks up the volume and overtakes the car in front of us.

—What now? I say.

—Where was that place? he says.

—Cumbria.

I've found an atlas and I rip out the page.

—Fuck it, why not, he says.

Ashley winds up the window. —Now do something useful.

—What?

He takes out his stash and throws it at me. —Skin up.

He takes out his box of Regal and some king size Rizla and throws them too. I look at the bag and the box and the papers, not really sure what to do with them. How difficult can it be? I think. And who cares, I've just seen my first red-backed shrike.

Kites

I don't think my mum knew that she liked women when she got with my dad. But I don't think she ever really liked men, so it was strange that she got with him in the first place. When I asked her about this, she said my dad was different to other men, but she didn't say how. So I don't know. I did try and ask her about him, but she blocked him out once he left. She didn't like me bringing him up so eventually I stopped. All I wanted to know was where he was. I wanted to write to him. She said she didn't know, and that was to be the end of it.

Things took a turn for the worse when I started puberty. It was quite odd really. I remember walking up the stairs to get something from my bedroom, and I shouted to my mum, — Won't be a minute, in my usual high-pitched voice. I think it was a jacket. I grabbed the jacket and was half way down the stairs when my mum shouts, —Have you got it? And I answer back, —Yes mum. But this 'yes mum' was really deep, I could feel it vibrate in my throat, it sort of tickled. It felt so weird, but that's when my voice broke aged thirteen, half way down the stairs.

By the time I was fourteen I was having to shave and my knob had got big. I started having really sexy thoughts all the time. And the only way to deal with them was to have a wank. Mum was seeing Tanya then, and Tanya had this habit of walking round naked. She had a really curvy figure and loads of hair around her fanny. Her breasts were really firm and her nipples seemed huge. I couldn't take my eyes off them when I saw them. And then I'd have to go to my room and knock one off. I think my mum cottoned on, because she and Tanya fell out. After that Tanya always wore a bathrobe if she wasn't dressed.

I was sitting reading one of my bird books in the kitchen, I looked up and my mum was staring at me. I asked her what the matter was, but she just shook her head. I kept seeing her doing it and in the end she told me. She said I was starting to look like my dad, I was even sounding like my dad, especially if she rang up and spoke to me on the phone. And my laugh, apparently my laugh is just like my dad's laugh, and my hands, the way I move them when I talk. The way I hold them when I think. But that can't really be my fault. I don't do it on purpose. Besides, I don't really remember his laugh, or his hands for that matter, so it's not like I'm copying off him.

But that's when it happened I think. This distance between us. We don't really talk any more and we don't go on holidays. Sometimes we watch TV together though, now that my sister's moved out. She moved out as soon as she turned sixteen. She's living with her boyfriend who mum doesn't like. Actually, I don't like him either. He's into sport.

—Pass it here, Ashley says. I pass him the spliff, which I admit, isn't great, but it's my third go at it and it will have to do. He takes it off me and looks at it with disapproval, but he lights it and smokes it nevertheless. He smiles. I smile back. We both nod our heads in time to the music.

—Why did you do it? I say.

—Do what?

—Why didn't you give that man the bag?

—It's time to branch out, he says. —Go it alone. As of today, I'm no longer Dave's oppo. He grins at me, but I'm not really sure about this.

I keep seeing Ashley close his eyes, which isn't a good sign, but I keep getting distracted by what's out of the window, which seems to be endlessly fascinating. I'm wondering how he can drive with his eyes closed. The car veers towards the barrier in the middle of the motorway. He opens them just in time and steers left. The car jerks.

—Where are we? Ashley shrugs. I look in the wing mirror and I don't like what I see.

—Oh no.

Dave is behind us in his smashed up car and he is gaining on us. Ashley sits up and puts his foot down and the car lurches forward. I look in the mirror again. Dave seems even closer.

—He's getting nearer.

—I'm going as fast as I can, Ashley says.

He's really put his foot down now but Dave is right behind us. Dave's car is much bigger than our car. I wonder if this is the right moment to suggest flight, but Ashley has an idea and he veers off the road, through a hedge, and across a ploughed field. The car churns up mud and we get about half way across the field when we come to a halt. We jump out, run across the field, but it's soft underfoot and progress is slow. We run into a wood. I turn around and see Dave's car pull up behind ours. He gets out. We run.

We've been running for about fifteen minutes. I'm tired and have to stop. I lean against a tree. Ashley stops too. We are both panting.

—Do you think we've lost him?

—Let's keep going.

—Look at the map.

—I reckon we're about here, I say, pointing at a pale grey bit of the map which should technically be a shade of green.

—Kendal's about ten miles this way, I say, pointing at the road going into Kendal which is pale green but should technically be a shade of grey.

—What's Kendal? he says.

—It's a town, we can hide there.

Ashley nods his head and we carry on through the woods, only walking this time. My coat feels heavy. I've got my field guide in my left pocket and my book on ravens in my right pocket. I'm sweating, but I don't want to take my coat off in case the books fall out. We walk for another mile or so and we come to the end of the woods. There's another field and then in the distance, a road. We head towards that.

When we get to the road, Ashley says, —We need some wheels.

We both look around but there are no cars.

—I think we've lost him, I say, looking back. We walk for about an hour but apart from a few farm buildings and dry stone walls, there's nothing. I don't even really see many birds. There are rooks in a field, and a wood pigeon, but that's about it. We see jackdaws further up, about four or five. They chase each other and tumble in flight. One of them lands close by, he walks and then hops.

A bit further on we see a kestrel. They're always a welcome sight. It rises up and then finds a place to hover. True hovering is lift generated through the bird alone, so it's usually only small birds that can do it. The largest bird that can truly hover is the pied kingfisher. Kestrels hover by flying into a headwind.

—Come on. We need to get a move on, I say. We've slowed down a bit, but it will be getting dark soon and we need to reach the town.

It takes us about another hour before we pass a sign that says: Welcome to Kendal. Kendal welcomes safe drivers. Ashley takes off his school tie and puts it in a bin nearby.

—We need to lose these, he says.

I take off my tie and put it in the bin too.

—We need to find somewhere to stay, I say, —Somewhere safe.

We carry on walking and pass Pizza Hut.

—Let's get something to eat, Ashley says. —I'm starving.

But I ignore him and we carry on walking.

—How much money have you got? I say.

He roots around in his pocket. —Enough.

Eventually I give in and we find a McDonald's. We order burgers, cokes and fries. We find somewhere to sit.

50

—So we lay low. Find somewhere to get our heads down. Then we move on in the morning. Ashley says. He eats his burger in four bites. He slurps his coke, then he starts on the fries. —Where though?

—Helvellyn, I say, straight away.

—Where's that?

I reach for the folded page of road atlas in my back pocket, but it's not there. Not a good sign. I take out the book on ravens and turn to the maps at the back. It shows where Helvellyn is in relation to Kendal.

—It's not far, I say.

We finish our food in silence.

—Watch this, Ashley says.

He gets up and approaches a six foot tall Ronald MacDonald clown. No one is looking so he picks it up.

—What you doing? I say.

But he's already by the door with the clown. A member of staff spots him and shouts. We both run out of the shop, Ashley carrying the clown, me still eating my burger. The man follows us out but we soon outrun him. We run down the street and round the corner. We collapse by some benches near the town hall. It is dusk. I'm wondering where we are going to stay tonight. I finish my burger as I watch the rooks above circling.

Above them in the distance I see a red kite soar, steering its course with its forked tail. It's too high up to make out its striking chestnut red belly, but you can just make out the white patches under its wings. Red kites have a high body-to-wingspan ratio. They can stay in the air for hours with hardly a beat of their wings.

—Let's get some booze, Ashley says.

But I don't respond. I'm just happy watching the rooks circle and the kite in the distance soaring above them.

Swifts

Swifts have sacrificed so much to be masters of the sky. They eat on the wing, breed on the wing, they even sleep on the wing. The swift's long scythe-like wings and forked tail are superbly adapted for flight. If they land on the ground they can't take off again. They are trapped. A young swift only gets one chance to become airborne. One chance. And if they don't make it, death.

It was when we were living in Ordsall in the flats. It felt funny to be living in a high-rise in Ordsall. They knocked most of them down, just kept that one, next to Ordsall Hall, called Nine Acre Court, so we got a good view of the estate. We were on the seventh floor so we were high up. You could see the Quays, all the new buildings and cranes. At night the light from the Quays made one half of the sky bright and the other dark. I found a grounded swift by the car park outside the health centre off Eccles New Road. It was in shock. I took it up to the flats and opened the window. I placed it on the palm of my hand and then I gently raised and lowered my arm. It was a mild evening and the sun was just going down. I let the bird feel the air under its wings. The bird came round from its shock then. It flapped its wings about and then just dropped off my hand and into the sky, flying up so that it was a black silhouette, like a boomerang. Lovely.

I'm thinking about this as we sit on the benches. There are a few swifts now, feeding on the flying insects that appear at dusk. The rooks have settled down for the night and the kite is nowhere to be seen. The way swifts feed is interesting. They have a special pouch at the back of their throats. They collect the insects as they fly, binding them together with saliva,

52

making a little food ball. These food balls can contain thousands of insects. I wouldn't fancy eating one myself though, not while we've still got McDonald's.

It's strange to see swifts in March, they don't usually arrive until late April. Then they're off again in July or August. They really just come to England to breed. There's no point in staying around after August because there are no insects. They go all the way to Africa, south of the Sahara, spend most of their year there, and then fly all the way back to England, just to breed. Fancy that.

Ashley went to get some booze nearly half an hour ago. I'm wondering where he's got to when he appears round the corner, empty handed.

—Fucking off-licences, he says.

He's tried three but was turned down at every one. I'm surprised. I think he could pass for eighteen, but apparently they all asked him for ID. It's getting ridiculous. You can't do anything. What's wrong with alcohol? It's mainly just water, with a few natural things added that make you feel good.

They tried to force feed us fruit at my last school. They were part of some council scheme. Every day a truck would come and deliver apples, oranges, bananas, all kinds of horrors. We were all told we had to eat one. We just took them out at break time and lobbed them over the science labs. It became a sport – how far can you throw a fruit. The teacher didn't understand why no one wanted bananas, but have you tried throwing a banana? They don't travel far at all, you're better off with an apple or, even better, an orange. You can throw an orange a fair old distance.

—Trouble, Ashley says.

I look up and see a group of five boys and three girls. They have spotted us and are walking across. Too late for us to run. The biggest one comes closer. He looks about seventeen, tall and rangy. He wears a white hooded top and a thick gold chain. Maybe it's not real gold.

53

—What you got there? he says to me, pointing at the Ronald McDonald I'm holding.

—What's it look like? Ashley says.

This white hooded top gives the rest of his gang a look, who are these people? The rest of the gang gather round. A girl with wavy brown hair walks up to me.

—Where you from? she says.

—What's it got to do with you?

I am wondering why Ashley doesn't shrink this white hooded boy like he did with the dull straw haired. Perhaps he is playing him along. The white hooded is a bit taller than Ashley and stockier, but I know that this won't faze Ashley.

—Watch it, he says.

—Salford, I say.

White hooded turns to me. —Where you going?

—Nowhere.

I look up at the sky again, slate grey clouds tinged yellow. A van pulls up with orange and red chevrons, it gives the white hooded a shock until he realises it's a gas van not the police.

—On holiday, I say. White hooded weighs me up. He looks at my school uniform, the mud on my shoes and trousers.

—Where you staying?

—A hotel.

—Come on, he says to his gang, and they start to move off.

—Wait.

He stops and moves back to us.

—What?

—Where you off? White hooded looks back at his gang, half-amused. Then he turns back to them and walks off.

The girl who quizzed me turns round, —Squat party, she says.

—Is that an invite?

The white hooded says straight away, —No chance.

He moves off again. The gang follow him.

—What about this lot? I say. I'm still holding Ashley's coat and I pull his stash from the inside pocket. White hooded looks at it and it dawns on him what it is. He smiles a big banana smile.

In a dark room staring at the girls. I look at my watch – just gone twelve. We still haven't got anywhere to stay, but I'm coming up on the second pill so my concern is very much in the background. First time I've had E – it's lovely. Orgasmic. Really happy and warm. White hooded is giving me a confrontational look, making me feel uneasy.

—Maybe we should go, I say.

—Nah, says Ashley.

—I'm not sure about this place.

Ashley takes out his bag of pills and necks another one. — Chill out, he says. He's sold quite a few at this party. The DJ is playing drum and bass and the bass is really distorted. The Ronald McDonald clown takes pride of place in front of the decks. He now wears a hat and holds some glow sticks. He has a Day-Glo whistle around his neck.

—Nice clown, says one of the girls to me. She is really pretty. I nod. She passes me a spliff and I take it off her.

—Thanks, I say.

—What's your name? She says.

—Cooper.

—I'm Becky.

She smiles and offers me her hand to shake. It feels warm and ever so slightly moist.

—It's a nice place this, I say. Just for something to say. Actually it's sparse and run-down. The plaster has come away in great chunks. The brickwork's exposed. It's a shit hole.

—It's alright, she says, looking around. —The squatters are always having parties.

I nod, and pass the spliff back. We stand and watch the dancers. There's a man with dreadlocks juggling luminous balls.

—So you're on holiday, she says.

—Yeah.

—Which hotel are you staying in?

—Er... I can't remember the name now.

She nods, then says, —You in trouble?

—What makes you say that?

Becky looks at me, cocks her head to one side like a dipper might do and I notice for the first time that she has bird-like eyes.

—What happened?

—What do you mean? She gives me that bird look again.

—Nothing, I say at last.

—You sure about that?

She looks at me suspiciously but then smiles.

—Bit of a man of mystery aren't you? she says.

I nod. I'm wondering if this is a good thing or a bad thing, but she smiled so it can't be bad. We sit in silence. I take out my book on ravens and pass it to her.

—I want to find some of these.

Becky looks through the book. Not like the way Ashley looked through it. She actually reads bits.

—You ever seen any?

—Only in films, she says. —What's that film with that bloke in it?

I shrug, because I don't know what she's talking about. —We had a school trip. Tower of London. I saw them there. Only they'd been clipped.

—How do you mean?

—They cut their wings so they can't fly off.

—That's cruel.

—I want to see them in the wild, I say.

—I've lived here all my life, she says, —and I've never seen them.

I take the book back off her and turn to the maps at the back, specifically to the map of Helvellyn.

—This is a good place to spot them, I say, pointing. —They're not easy to find. Farmers shoot them. So they keep themselves to themselves.

—And you've come all this way, just to see them?

—Yep.

—That's a bit odd.

We sit in silence, but it's not uncomfortable. Her thigh is pressed against my thigh. I can feel its warmth and electricity. The drugs are strong. I feel like we are practically having sex, just sitting here.

—So what do you want to do? I say finally.

—Now?

—With your life.

—I'm going to be a doctor.

Not, I want to be a doctor, but I'm going to be a doctor. Just like that.

—Yeah, right, I say.

—What's so funny about that?

—I want to be ruler of the world, I say.

I don't want to be ruler of the world as it happens. I want to go to bed with Becky with no clothes on and feel her and be inside her. But I don't tell her that.

—I'm serious, she says.

We sit in silence again and I'm enjoying being close to her. Then she reaches over to me and kisses me.

Things blur. Hip flesh, thumping beat. The white hooded, Ashley. Thump thump. Then she's dragging me away.

Penguins

There's a good argument, and it's been made before, so I won't go on about it, for the elimination of pandas. I don't mean we actually actively all go out now and hunt down a panda, just withdrawing the support we have offered so far and letting nature take its course – in other words, let them die out naturally, as they would do if it wasn't for us. It's a sensitive subject and people get emotional about it, but the history of evolution is full of extinct species. Every day, several hundred species die out. Well, maybe not several hundred – I mean, it might be more, it might be less. I've no idea. The point is, no one cares about them. But pandas, people get soft.

The giant panda I'm talking about, the one with the black eyes. If you are going to restrict your diet to bamboo – which isn't a bright move – you are signing your own suicide note. Bamboo is not a highly nutritious food, it contains barely any nutrition at all, and this means that the panda needs to spend all of its waking day eating. While it is eating the bamboo, do you ever think it passes a yam or an orange, and thinks, maybe I'll have a change today, give something new a try? It's a logical thought – but not to the panda. There are currently 1,590 pandas living in the wild. This number is on the rise because we keep extracting semen from male pandas in captivity and using it to artificially inseminate female pandas.

Male pandas don't fancy female pandas. Basically, they don't want to get it on with them. Taxonomically the panda is classed as a carnivore, it's a bear after all, let's not forget that. So why have humans put such effort into sustaining an evolutionary mistake, while all about us thousands of species perish? Simple.

The panda, as my mum is fond of telling me, is cute. It looks like a big cuddly baby.

We have spent so much time and effort encouraging them to mate. This includes, showing them videos of mating pandas and giving male pandas Viagra. That's right, we've brought them into captivity to show them panda porn and give them drugs. On top of this, a female panda is only fertile for two or three days a year. To add to this, a female panda, if she has two cubs, will normally abandon one of them. And the father has no part in helping to raise the cub. From the moment the cub is born, its mum will abandon it for up to four hours a day.

You don't get snow leopards behaving like that, or the golden lion tamarind – but no one gives a monkeys about them. But they are both equally as threatened as the giant panda. The pig-footed bandicoot, the giant tree rat, the emperor rat, the bulldog rat – in fact lots of rats, the big eared hopping mouse, the dusky flying fox, the sea mink, the Javan tiger, the Japanese wolf, the Barbary lion – all extinct in recent times. As for birds, since the sixteenth century, 140 bird species have become extinct.

The penguin, like the panda, should just die. This bird spent millions of years evolving the ability to fly only to spend the next million or so years evolving the ability to *not* fly – and it has chosen to live on a lump of ice. It spends half the year sitting on an egg in sub-zero temperatures, and the other half of the year abandoning its mate to get food. That's a pretty stupid way to live your life. I'm not saying sitting on your arse watching Jeremy Kyle while stuffing Doritos down your gullet is any better, but you see my point.

There's a film called March of the Penguins. My mum got it out on DVD for us last year. I think it was the last time we sat down and watched something together. It was just before she got with Heather. She'd just broken up with Tanya.

She came in one day with a KFC family bucket, six tins of lager, and the DVD of March of the Penguins.

—I've had a really tough day at work, she said. —Let's just veg out.

So we did. She explained that she'd got us a film about birds to watch, —so you'll like it, she said. As if that was the final word on the subject. As soon as the film started, I could feel my irritation begin to build. It was the soundtrack, horrible weepy music that kept building up at points of high emotion. Then there was Morgan Freeman's narration – he spoke about penguins as though they were humans. Penguins are not humans.

There are basically two reasons the film did so well in America – one, it promoted conservative family values, and two, it made penguins look cute. Oh, and a third reason, Americans are wankers. When the penguin chick died, my mum wept into our KFC bucket. I had to fetch tissues. Uncontrollable weeping. Pathetic. And some of the respect I had for my mother died that day. When Morgan says, 'in the harshest place on Earth, love finds a way', I could have kicked my foot through the television. 'Love', how can you talk about penguins being in love?

I suppose at about the same time, last year or thereabouts, I skipped double maths followed by PE to go into town to watch a film. I went on my own. It was a film about grizzly bears. This stupid American bloke had filmed himself getting close to grizzly bears for years. At the end of the film, the bears attack and eat him. The camera goes black and we just hear the sound of bears eating him. At this point, a man sitting in front of me burst out laughing. He thought it was a spoof documentary and was shocked when he realised it was real.

—What you laughing about, Ashley says, as we approach Becky's place. It's dark but there's a light outside the porch, a sort of lantern. It's the same type as the one in Larder's cafe in Salford precinct, although it doesn't have a big smiley face on it and it doesn't look out of place here. The house is massive with huge iron gates. Becky has to punch a number into a keypad for the gates to open, like you see in films. It's a bit like that house in Emmerdale where those posh people live.

I smile at Ashley. I am very high. We've been walking for about half an hour but it could be two minutes or an hour, I've really no idea. It doesn't feel like walking, more like gliding, like a gull coming into land, almost skimming the crust of the earth. I can still hear the thud of the music in my ears even though we are a long way from the squat party now. She leads us through this grand hallway. There's a large staircase, marble and statues. There are large oil paintings on the wall, blocks of colour and squiggles. Some of them look as if they haven't been finished, hurried yellow brush strokes and dribbles of loose red paint.

—You live here?

—What's so strange about that? she says.

—So what does your dad do then?

—He's a civil engineer.

—It must pay well, I say.

—Actually, mum's the breadwinner. She's a barrister.

Ashley gives me a look. I just shrug. I've heard the word before on TV but don't know what one is.

—Where are they now? I say.

—They're away for a few days.

Ashley gives me a nod. I smile back. We're in.

The living room. The floor is bare wood, no carpets, just a rug, a cream rug. A cream rug, mum wouldn't like that, she tends to go with patterned carpet, says it hides the sins of the world. There's this semi-circular cream-coloured leather sofa, a shade darker than the rug, and a huge wood-burning open fire in the middle of the room, although the fire isn't lit. I sit down on the sofa.

Ashley walks around, picking up ornaments and turning them round in his hands. He seems impressed by their weight, as if that's how you measure whether it's a good ornament or a shit one. Becky enters with two ruby coloured drinks in tall chunky glasses. She hands one to me. Ashley must have told

61

her he didn't want one because he doesn't seem to mind being left out. He stares around the room, a bit puzzled. Becky takes a sip of her drink.

I watch Ashley pace the room, searching round for something. He turns to me, his brow creased in confusion. —Where's the television? he says. I just shrug, how should I know?

—Actually, I'm quite tired, Becky says. She yawns, then puts a hand over her mouth. —I'll show you to your room if that's ok?

Ashley shrugs and I nod. She leads us back into the hallway and up the staircase to a room and opens the door. She switches the light on. There's a single bed in one corner and an armchair. There's a bookcase stuffed full of books. It's a small room, I'm thinking, for the both of us. Ashley bags the bed straight away and I'm wondering where I'm going to sleep. He bounces up and down on the mattress looking smug. There's only really the armchair and I don't fancy that. It looks quite hard and there are no cushions. I suppose there's the floor. Then Becky opens up a cupboard and grabs a light bulb. She turns round and leads me down the landing.

We stop about three or four rooms down from Ashley's and she opens a door. There's a double bed and a lounge area with a sofa and TV and DVD. There's even a sink and a toilet and a shower to one side. It's about the same size as my living room at home plus my mum's bedroom and mine put together. She puts the bulb in the lamp next to the bed and turns it on.

—You can sleep here, she says.

I don't quite understand why I get such a big room, so I say, —Where are you going to sleep?

She closes the door behind us and locks it. She takes my drink off me and puts both our drinks on the table. She starts to kiss me. She pulls off her vest top. She unfastens her bra. She throws it in the corner and kisses me again. Becky turns off the big light and the room suddenly feels smaller and warmer. She leads me to the bed, we fall onto it and I feel like I'm lying on a cloud and drifting through the sky.

Cuckoos

The chiffchaff is a warbler, very much like a willow warbler only it's not quite as yellow. I've mistaken the chiffchaff for the willow warbler on a number of occasions now. Unless you are quite close up, the only real definite way of telling them apart is through their song. The chiffchaff is named after its song, so that's easy to remember. But I've listened to the song of the chiffchaff many times and I don't think it sounds like 'chiffchaff' at all. I think it sounds like 'chick-chick-chick-chick-chick-chick-chick-chack-chick-chick-chick'. It's lovely but that would be a very long name for a bird.

There are a number of birds that have onomatopoeic names. The obvious one is the cuckoo. I've never seen a cuckoo, but I have heard one several times. They have quite a sleek body and a long tail. They get a bit of bad press because they are technically parasites. But it makes a lot of sense if you think about it, I mean why spend all that effort making your own nest and catching your own food to feed your young when you can get someone else to do it? I actually find myself admiring them. The adult cuckoos should be arriving back from Africa around this time, they stop here for the summer, so I might even see one in Cumbria if I'm lucky.

The reason why I'm on the side of the cuckoo is that when a cuckoo puts its egg in another bird's nest it is usually a much smaller bird and the rest of the eggs are half the size, so it's the other bird's fault. When the cuckoo chick hatches, it grows much bigger and looks so different to the other birds, that you've got to wonder about how smart the parents of those birds are. It hatches earlier, the chick grows faster, then starts kicking the rest of the chicks out of the nest. How many clues do you want?

My mum's brother, not her scary brother Tony, but her youngest brother, my uncle Mark, is a bit of a cuckoo, so my mum says. He used to pop round for a cuppa every now and again. Just pop his head in on the way to the pub, as though five floors up he could just be passing by, and ask if the kettle had just boiled. He'd never say much, used to just sit on the sofa watching telly. Then he'd finish his tea, say it was lovely and he'd be off down the Brown Cow or the Black Horse.

He came round about four years ago when his wife kicked him out, asked if he could kip for the night. He slept on the sofa in our flat in Ordsall. Then the next night, he somehow persuaded mum to let him stay again. This went on for about three weeks, it wound my sister up so much, she went to stay at her mate's, so Mark moved into my sister's bedroom. My mum started shouting at him, but he said that there was no point him sleeping on the sofa when there was a bed going spare. I could see his point but my mum blew her top and kicked him out. He rarely comes round now.

They say when you hear a cuckoo, that's when spring starts. For some reason it often lays in the reed warbler's nest, which is quite funny really. Maybe the reed warbler is a particularly stupid bird and that's why the cuckoo picks on it. When the female reed warbler lays her eggs, the female cuckoo waits for her to fly off, then she flies into the nest, kicks one of the eggs out and lays her own egg. She can do this in almost no time at all. You have to have some admiration for anything that sneaky. There are a lot of blokes in Salford like that.

It's a funny thing with onomatopoeia because it's a bit of a myth. I mean a dog doesn't really go woof, does it? It sort of goes 'rrrrrrrrrrruuuuuuuuuuff'. Only the 'r' sound sort of darkens as it builds. As though it were taking the 'r' sound from the front of its mouth to the back of its throat. I watched a programme about it on daytime TV. They show some good educational programmes on BBC during the day so it makes sense to stay off school and watch television instead. Anyway, apparently in Japan, they say 'wan wan' instead of 'woof' which isn't even close. And in France they go 'ouaf ouaf' which is just daft. In Spain they go 'guau guau', which is even more ridiculous – if I were a dog I'd be insulted by that.

They sell Rice Krispies on the TV by saying they go 'snap, crackle and pop', but they don't go 'snap, crackle and pop' at all, in fact they don't go anything like that. I know, I've listened to them a lot. Now the cuckoo doesn't really go 'cuckoo'. I'd say it goes more like 'wah-hoo, wah-hoo'. But I suppose it's debatable, and 'cuckoo' is certainly closer to its call than 'chiffchaff' is to a chiffchaff's. You get it a lot in comic books – onomatopoeia I'm talking about now, not cuckoos. Wham, biff, smack – stuff like that. My favourite is the sound of Spider-Man's web shooter in the Marvel comics, which is written as, 'thwip!'. It always makes me laugh, that.

Becky is fast asleep beside me. Her hair is a dark chestnut brown, the same colour as a dipper's belly only with more of a sheen, and her skin is really creamy, almost white, like the dipper's breast. I can't sleep at all. Must be all the drugs. I'm just lying here watching her and letting my mind drift from one thought to another. Like a warm bath for your mind. You can just let your mind soak in all those bubbly thoughts. I think about Ashley. I wonder if he's asleep. He's probably helping himself to the drinks cabinet. I saw him eyeing it up earlier. Or maybe he is helping himself to some stuff, small ornaments or jewellery – stuff that he can put into his pocket.

Then I think about Dave. I think about everything that has happened today. It would make for an extended episode of The Met. I went to school, then we met Dave. Then Dave's brother ripped Ashley's fingernail off with a pair of long-nose pliers that reminded me of a snipe's bill. Thinking about it some more, I'd say the truer resemblance was to an oystercatcher's bill – in shape, not colour. An oystercatcher's bill is bright orange.

65

Whereas the bill of a pair of long-nose pliers is a sort of dull grey-silver.

That doesn't really matter. Then we ran away, then we stole a car and knocked Andy down. The car really smashed into him and there was blood everywhere. I wouldn't say he was alright. I'd say he was dead. That would explain Dave's look. Then we had a car chase. I tried to shoot Dave. Then we walked into Kendal. Then we nicked a clown, went to a squat party, took lots of drugs and I ended up here and had sex for the first time ever with Becky, who is lovely. Not bad. Thinking about it, you'd probably need to stretch that over three or four episodes of The Met.

Since meeting Ashley, my life has definitely got more interesting. I've done a lot of things I've never done before.

So what is Dave going to do about Andy? What would I do? If someone killed my sister, I don't think I'd actually do anything. If we still lived in the flat in Ordsall, I would have moved into her bedroom, like my uncle Mark did, because her room was bigger than mine, not that she had any more space though, because she filled her room with blank staring dolls. I need to think like Dave. What would Dave do? What *did* Dave do? Dave chased us all the way up to Cumbria in a smashed up car with no windscreen. Then he chased us across the ploughed field. This makes me think Dave is not happy. We lost him in the woods, but what's bothering me is that he would have got to the road eventually, same as us.

Something else is bothering me. I lost the map out of my back pocket. If Dave picked that map up he will have seen that I drew a line from the motorway we were on all the way across to Kendal. I also drew a big circle round the word, 'Kendal.' So even a reed warbler would be able to work that one out. We put our school ties in the bin close to the sign that said 'Welcome to Kendal.' So if he did get to Kendal he'd probably see them and know we are here. This isn't good.

He's more than likely to ring up his mates and get them to drive across here. They are probably prowling the streets now. At least he won't be able to find Becky's place. How would he? He'll prowl around and probably look for boys about our age. Maybe he'll stop the car and ask them if they've seen us. But who will he stop at this time of night? Perhaps a gang coming out of a squat party. Oh dear. What if he stops the white hooded's gang? But why would they tell him anything? Well, maybe white hooded would because he was pissed off with us. He saw us leave with Becky. But does he know where Becky lives? Course he must do, this place is a palace.

I'm starting to panic now. My mind is going round and round, my pulse is racing, and I can't get the image of Dave's face out of my mind, staring back at me with the body of his brother next to him. Andy's body, limp and wet with blood. Stop, calm down, try and think calm thoughts. I go through all the warblers. First there's the swamp warblers: the rather stupid reed warbler, the great reed, marsh, river, Cetti's, Savi's. What are the other ones? Sedge, moustached, grasshopper, aquatic, fan-tailed. Then there's the scrub warblers: the blackcap, the whitethroat, the lesser whitethroat, spectacled, Dartford, barred... Can't remember the others. Missed quite a few there. Then there's all the leaf warblers: willow, chiffchaff, arctic, greenish, yellow-browed, wood, olive-tree, garden, melodious... what's the one I always forget?

Roadrunners

Takes a while to remember where I am. Sun streams through the blinded window in shafts of light. I look round but nothing seems familiar. Then I see Becky lying next to me and all the memories of last night come flooding back. I study her features, her unblemished cheek, her ruffled hair, the smooth, sleek skin of her shoulders. The curve of her eyelashes, the soft pink lobe of flesh beneath her ear, the fine, almost invisible hairs on her neck. I look around the room, our clothes lying crumpled on the floor, the red foil wrapper, our drinks on the table by the door, unfinished.

Now I notice the book shelves for the first time. Becky has loads of books, crammed into the shelves, things you'd expect to find on there like Harry Potter books and Stephen King, but also lots of more interesting material. A book called Dark Music catches my eye and so does one called Meltdown, but they look like novels. Becky opens her eyes and looks over at me. She smiles and sits up.

—Morning, she says. But it's actually afternoon. —Did you sleep ok? I nod, and stare out of the window. Now it feels weird being in bed with her. Now I'm aware of how real she is, of how naked she is, and of how naked I am.

—So what do you want to do today? she says.

—I don't know, I finally manage.

—I thought you wanted to find those ravens?

—Maybe.

—Show me the map.

I look over to where my clothes are, my boxers entangled where I threw them last night. I try to appear casual as I hop out of bed, grabbing my boxers and pulling them on. I find my jacket and reach into the pocket. I take out the book on ravens and sit on the bed. She takes the book. She opens it at the back where the maps of breeding pair nesting sites are. I've ringed the one of Helvellyn.

—Is this the place?

—Yeah.

She looks through the book some more and as she does the photograph of me and my dad with the stuffed raven falls on to the bed. She picks it up.

—Is that your dad? I nod. —Where is he now? I shrug. — Don't you know?

I don't manage to say anything for a long time. My mouth goes dry. Then I answer her, —That's all I have.

She goes to turn the photograph over but I snatch it off her before she has chance to do this.

—What's the matter?

I put the photograph back in the book and close the book over it. I'm aware of Becky staring at me, then she strokes my cheek and gives me a hug.

—We'll find these birds, she says.

—Are you coming then?

—They're away for a few days she says, meaning her parents. —It's a bit boring round here. Why not?

She goes over to her wardrobe and takes out some binoculars – a pair of Viking 10 x 42 Navigators. They cost nearly two hundred pounds. They're nitrogen-filled to prevent condensation and are one hundred percent waterproof. She tells me her dad gave them her, but she's hardly ever used them.

—Can I try them? She hands them to me. They feel lovely. I hold them to my eyes and bring the world outside into focus, blurring the blinds in the foreground. I hand them back. She takes out a black rucksack and packs a few things, make-up, clothes, she throws in the binoculars, as though they were any pair of binoculars. We both get dressed. I'm fully dressed now and Becky is putting on a clean vest top from a drawer and putting it on over her bra. She goes into the bathroom. I can hear the clack of glass on tiles, then the sound of water running. There's a bang on the door. I open it.

Ashley's in a bit of a state. I ask him what the matter is. When he woke up he felt a bit groggy, he says, so he went downstairs and found some headache tablets in the kitchen. He poured himself a glass of water and went outside to get some fresh air. That's when he saw it, a blue car with Dave, and some other boys. Ashley knew the boy who was driving, someone called Sean, and he's bad news according to Ashley.

—Did they see you?

He shakes his head, he doesn't think so, but we need to go. If they've been given our address by the white hooded or some of the others, they'll be here soon. He goes back downstairs and I decide to follow him. We go outside and have a walk round the garden, keeping close to the hedges. We peep at the road, but there's just a few parked cars. A chaffinch hops about, nest building, with a bit of dried grass in his mouth. The men with the strimmers have been and all the grass verges between the pavement and the road have been cut. A paper boy passes with a fluorescent bag and disturbs the bird – it flies off

—Come on, Ashley says, and we edge round the back. There's a driveway covered with trees and bushes. Ashley scans the cars. He finds one he can manage, but then says, —You have a go. At first I think, no way, but then, why not?

I leave Ashley in the back of the car, keeping an eye out. I go back to Becky. I find Ashley's blazer, I'm about to pick it up, but think it's better if he doesn't wear it. I reach into the inside pocket though and take out the bag of drugs, don't want to be leaving that behind. I go up the stairs and into Becky's bedroom. She wants to know where I've been. I think about telling her about the trouble we're in but decide against it. As far as Becky's concerned we are just going raven spotting, best to keep it at that. She has her bag packed. We go down into the kitchen and she takes out a bottle of juice, sliced meat and cheese. She goes to the cupboard and takes out a small loaf of bread, chocolate and crisps. She throws all this into the rucksack.

—Can you drive? Becky says.

—I've got us a car. We go outside and I lead her to where I've parked up in a secluded spot. I start the engine and give it some revs. I think about telling Becky about Dave again, but I look at Ashley through the rear-view mirror and he is shaking his head.

I tell Becky that Helvellyn will be a good place to find the ravens and she shuffles through the pages of a road atlas that was crammed into the passenger seat back pocket. We drive up to Helvellyn. Becky wants to know where we're going to stay. It's a good question and I look to Ashley for an answer but he just shrugs his shoulders. I drive the car around for a while, keeping an eye out. I take Ashley's silence for worry. He's worried about Dave, but I can't reassure him without giving the game away to Becky. But there's no way Dave will know where we are. I want to tell Becky about Dave, it's not nice to keep things from her, but it's the best way. In any case, this is fun, driving around. The thing about The Met is that it's set in London, which is boring. The scenery around here is more dramatic. Perhaps I should write to them and suggest changing location.

All this running away from Dave reminds me of the Road Runner cartoon. I used to watch it a lot on Cartoon Network when we had Sky, before they cut us off. Now we've just got freeview, which is rubbish for cartoons. You can watch it on YouTube but I got my computer taken off me. Some men came one day, just before we left Ordsall, and took my Xbox, my computer and some of my mum's jewellery, including her wedding ring, which she said she was glad to get rid of. But she was crying, so maybe she didn't mean that. What I liked about Road Runner was the Wile E. Coyote character. Coyotes sometimes get mistaken for wolves, but they are really more like a jackal. I don't think they actually eat roadrunners in reality, although Wile E. Coyote never actually catches the roadrunner either, so this is true to life.

I don't mind so much that cartoons always anthropomorphise animals. It's understandable. It's just when they put human emotions onto real animals, like Morgan Freeman does in March of the Penguins – I don't like that because they were real penguins. No one thinks Mickey Mouse is a real mouse, and no one thinks Road Runner is a real roadrunner. A roadrunner can outrun a rattlesnake – and will eat one if it gets the chance. There can't be many animals hard enough to eat rattlesnakes. They can run up to 17mph, which is pretty good for a bird. They prefer running to flying and are actually in the same family as cuckoos. Like cuckoos, some roadrunners like to lay their eggs in other birds' nests. Warner Bros were right to portray them as outsmarting the coyote because, like cuckoos, they are incredibly sneaky. Wile E. Coyote should give up and catch squirrels or voles – something he's actually got a chance of catching.

But I like that. I like the fact that he never gives up and I like the fact he is trying to catch something he will never catch. We can all relate to that. In our case, Dave is Wile E. Coyote and we are the roadrunner, although I don't think we are as smart as the roadrunner and this concerns me. There is a clip on YouTube where the roadrunner finally gets caught by Wile E. Coyote. He shakes him, kicks him, then stamps on him, then he lets a truck drive over him and then finally he straps him to a large stick of dynamite and fires him off into the sky. But I don't think this is an official clip – I think someone has done a pirate version because the drawing isn't quite right.

It's important for some reason that the roadrunner is never caught, so whoever did the pirate version should be ashamed of themselves. The Warner Bros cartoon characters were always more interesting than Disney. Warner Bros invented Wile E. Coyote, Road Runner, Bugs Bunny, Daffy Duck and Sylvester the cat. Disney invented Mickey Mouse, Pluto, Donald Duck and Goofy. If you put Warner Bros characters against Disney cartoon characters in a fight, Warner Bros would win every time. Similarly, if you wanted to have a laugh, you wouldn't hang around with Mickey and his gang of feeble dimwits, you'd go straight to Bugs Bunny or Daffy Duck.

Like the roadrunner bird in the cartoon, it's important that we don't get caught, as Dave and this Sean are sure to find their own way of kicking us, stamping on us, driving over us and finally blowing us to pieces. I just hope we are Warner Bros characters and not a set of feeble Disney characters.

We've been driving around for several hours now. Becky suggested we stay in a B and B but Ashley doesn't like this idea. I'm actually able to talk to Ashley now without using my voice, so we can discuss Becky without her knowing, which seems a bit mean, but it's for her own good. I try to convince Ashley that we should tell Becky what's happened, but he says I'm not to. We have parked up by a wood and Ashley has gone for a walk to see if he can find somewhere. I can't talk to him from this distance, so I tell Becky to wait in the car a moment while I have a look for him.

I find him scrambling up a bit of loose scree. We have to use the roots of trees to climb the slope.

—I can tell Becky exactly what happened, I say. —I think she'd be ok with it. She's been ok with the drugs and nicking a car so I think she'd be ok with Dave.

—Did you fuck her?

—Yes.

—Liar.

We sit down at the top of the scree to get our breath back.

—I don't care, she's a fat minger, he says.

I think about punching him, but he says —You better not even try it.

How did he know I was going to hit him?

—I know everything you're thinking, he says.

—No you don't, I say.

—Listen, I know you fucked her, alright, and I'm not bothered, I've fucked loads of girls and they were all fitter than her. I'll tell you something else.

—What?

—You're a fucking nutter.

—How do you make that out?

—All that stuff about long-nose pliers reminding you of one sort of bird then another, do you think that's normal, you spaz?

—It was the bill of a snipe, I say, —then a woodcock. But while Becky was sleeping, I realised it was more like the bill of an oystercatcher.

—Stop going on about birds, he says, —I don't care.

He gets up and wanders off. I look around at the trees and the undergrowth. I think I see a treecreeper on the trunk of a sycamore but I need the binoculars to make it out properly. I do see a pied flycatcher though, a female, which isn't as striking as the male, more brown than black, although it has the same wing markings. I could really do with Becky's binoculars. They have a really impressive field of view and are a good weight and size. It felt nice to hold them in her bedroom, to cup the moulded body in my hands and feel the rubber lips of the lens-protectors mouth my eye sockets.

The flycatcher forages for insects on the ground, finds a grub and then flies off. My binoculars are a pair of Praktica Zooms from Argos. My mum bought them for my birthday a few years ago, although I chose them myself. As I scan the hedgerows, I spot something else, Ashley is walking towards me.

—Come on, he says.

—Have you found somewhere?

—Yep.

I get up and brush the bits of branches and leaves off my trousers.

—Hang on, I say, —I'll get Becky.

He nods reluctantly and leans against a tree, almost as if he's entertaining the idea of leaving her behind.

The Nuthatch

We trudge across barren moorland. The ground is uneven and muddy in places. It's not much of a path, more a rabbit run. We've been walking for about twenty minutes in almost complete silence. I'm thinking already that this is going to be a good place to find ravens. They seem to thrive the further they are away from humans. There are lots of tall trees and rugged crags, ideal habitat. We don't see any though, just crows, jackdaws and rooks. I'm getting quite irritated by crows now. When we were at the Tower of London, it was easy to distinguish between a crow and a raven because close up you can see that crows are much smaller. But here on these moors, the birds are much further away. We walk towards a desolate shack.

—Is this it? I say to Ashley without talking. I'm a bit disappointed. Becky has hardly said anything at all.

—Wait till you see inside, Ashley says.

We carry on walking until we arrive at the entrance of the hut. I open the door and we go inside. It's dark and takes us a few moments for our eyes to adjust. Ashley opens his arms out, by way of introduction to the place. It's small. There's a mattress in one corner with some blankets heaped on top. There's a table, a sink and some kitchen units. There's a black pot-bellied stove in the middle of the room with a kettle on top and an old rocking chair close by. It's cosier on the inside than it looks from the outside, but it still looks fairly bleak.

—What do you think? Ashley says.

Becky looks around, —It's a bit small, she says.

—Where we going to sleep? I say.

Ashley looks around. —Well, I suppose you and Becky can have the mattress. I can sleep in the chair.

Becky doesn't hear him, and I wish he'd start talking properly, it seems mean to keep her out. She goes to the cupboards and opens them. There are a few chipped enamel plates and mugs. There's a cutlery drawer and a cupboard with some pans in. She finds a pile of chopped logs in a wooden crate.

—We can have a cuppa.

—What with?

We look in the cupboards some more. There is a tin of tuna that has rusted and looks very old. She holds the tin up and I wince. I've always had this thing about tinned tuna, I'm not really sure why but I think it's to do with opening the can and seeing the moist flesh of the fish exposed, swimming in brine, like the flotsam of an aquatic disaster.

—There's no milk, no water, and no teabags, she says. Although we all know this.

—There was a shop about two or three miles down the road, Ashley says.

We look around some more.

—How do you know someone doesn't already live here?

Ashley looks around and shrugs. —There'd be more stuff, he says. He picks up the tin of tuna. —I mean, this is ancient. It can't have been lived in for years.

Becky raises her eyebrows, unsure.

—It's better than a Youth Hostel or a Bed and Breakfast, I say, picking up on Becky's look.

—How do you work that out? she says.

—He's right, Ashley says. —It's better than them places.

I know what he is thinking, that those are the sort of places Dave will check out, but he doesn't let on about Dave to Becky.

—It will do for now, she says. I go over to the mattress. I pick up one of the blankets and sniff. It doesn't smell great. Ashley's by the pot-bellied stove. He opens the door and pokes about with a metal rod. Becky goes to the cupboards again and carries on searching. She goes to the sink and looks out of the window.

—Shit! Someone's coming, she says.

We freeze in panic. I grab Becky and we duck behind some cupboards. Ashley takes the poker he's been using and takes position behind the door. He holds the poker above his head.

The door opens and in walks a man. He looks about sixty and is very large. About six foot three maybe and heavily built. He has a massive head, which is shaven, although there's a lot of black and white stubble on top of his head and around his jaw. He has very prominent scars on his face, two deep ridges of scar tissue curl up at either side of his mouth, travelling up his cheeks almost towards his ears, which makes him look like he is grimacing. He wears a big black overcoat and has a plastic shopping bag in each hand. His hands are huge. He plonks the bags in the middle of the room.

Ashley creeps up behind him. We watch from behind the cupboards. He holds the poker and is about to cosh the man, when this man turns around just in time and ducks out of the way. He grabs Ashley's arm and wrestles the poker off him. He throws Ashley to the ground. He strikes him repeatedly with the poker until Ashley's head explodes and bits of skull and brain and blood spurt all over the room. No, the man hasn't noticed Ashley, so I jump out holding a frying pan.

—Argghh! I shout.

The man turns to us now and sees me and Becky.

—Who the fuck are you? he says.

—Who the fuck are *you*? Ashley says.

The man laughs. —What the fuck are you doing in my house? he says. —You've got a fucking cheek ant you?

He approaches me and holds up the poker. He's about to whack me.

—Wait! I shout. —We made a mistake. We thought this place was empty.

The man considers this. He lowers the poker.

—Well it ain't. Now clear off.

Me and Becky edge towards the door but Ashley approaches the man. —Look, we're really sorry about that, he says.

The man ignores him. —Go on, do one, he says. Ashley edges towards the door too but then turns back to the man.

—Don't suppose there's any chance of a cuppa? he says to the man.

That's actually not a bad idea, I could do with a cup of tea. Becky pulls at my sleeve. The man stares back as though he can't believe I'm standing in his doorway, then he charges at us. We run out the door.

We run a few hundred yards, but when we look back, the man hasn't followed us. There's just the dull windows of the shack staring blankly out.

—So what now? Becky says.

We sit down by some rocks, on the outskirts of the trees. Still no sign of any ravens. I take the binoculars and have a look. I search the outline of the trees. There's a wren in the shadow of a boulder, hopping about, its comparatively long tail bobbing up and down. It sticks its bill into a fissure in the rock. A dunnock lands nearby and close to this a robin perches on a broken branch, its bright orangey-red breast still visible in the darkness beneath the tree's canopy.

The robin's reputation as being cute has always amused me, in fact it is a very aggressive bird. I remember a teacher called Mrs Woods in primary school telling us about a robin that used to follow her as she walked her dog along a footpath near where she lived. How friendly it is, she said. It's not being friendly, I pointed out, you are on its patch and it is warning you off. She didn't believe me, but a male robin will happily peck a rival male to death if it wanders into its territory. This robin watches the wren suspiciously, but the wren, probably all too aware of the robin's ruthlessness, flies off.

I'm sure that a lot of the misunderstanding about the robin's behaviour is down to that story we were told at school about a robin visiting Christ on the cross. According to the story, as Jesus was strung out dying, a robin came and sang in his ear to soothe him and the blood from his wounds stained the robin's breast. And they actually expect you to learn things at school?

Apparently the robin is the most popular bird in Britain. There was a campaign a few years ago to make it the official national bird. Perhaps, given the national pastime of men fighting outside pubs of an evening, it would be an apt choice.

The robin flies off, then there's nothing for a while, just the leaves flapping and some grass swaying slightly in the weak breeze. Then I see the dunnock again. It doesn't stay long, it shows some interest in some of the undergrowth, pecking at some moss, then it flies off too. Then there's nothing for a good few minutes. Becky fiddles with the zip on her coat, turning the metal clasp around and rubbing its smoothness with her thumb and index finger. Ashley puts his hands in his pockets and stares at the ground. He kicks a twig about and scuffs up some undergrowth. I take up the binoculars again and scan the line of trees. Then I see it, by the side of a tree trunk, what looks like a small woodpecker. I focus in on it, zooming in on its striking colouring, a sort of blue-grey upper body with buff under-parts and orangey chestnut flanks. Its cheeks are white with a bold black streak through its eyes. It climbs the tree in short jerky motions. It's a nuthatch.

The first time I saw a nuthatch was when we went to Nottingham. My mum had to have an operation and we drove down with this woman she was seeing at the time called Susan. I must have been eight or nine. I was never told what the operation was for, but she'd been in a lot of pain for quite a long time and she'd be really moody for days, snapping at us. My sister was at school. I can't remember why I wasn't at school. I think it must have been one of the times I was excluded for not turning up to class, which I always think is a strange punishment. I got into the habit of going to Central Library in Manchester every morning instead of school. It was easy, you just had to stay on the bus until it got to the end of the route rather than getting off before. I'd go to the ornithological section and read books and make notes. I'd take my sketchbook and do some drawings. I could spend all day there and usually did.

The ornithological section was only small, really just two or three shelves. It was sandwiched between ants and rats in the main reading room, a massive dome, like being inside a giant's skull. There was a hole at the top where light came in so that you got natural light for reading. It was like the giant's eye, a Cyclops, an eye not peering out at the world but peering in. There were some words going all the way round the room in a big circle. Something about getting wisdom and embracing her like wisdom was a woman. Strange acoustics in there. You could hear someone at the opposite end of the room better than someone a few feet away. Someone at the opposite end of the room cutting paper sounded alien and strange and wonderful. Even someone turning the pages of a book sounded like something from Doctor Who.

I'd only meant to go there for a few days, but before you know it, I hadn't been to school for nearly a month. They'd written to my mum a few times but I'd seen the letters on the mat and put them in the bin before she got to them. Anyway, it was a nice day out. I'd never been to Nottingham before. Susan said that they'd have to keep her in overnight, so we stayed at a B and B. I don't remember that, but I do remember having a walk in the wood with Susan and spotting a nuthatch. My first nuthatch. This was before I had my field guide with its definitive list. I had my Usborne Spotter's Guide which I'd bought myself for Christmas with a token my uncle Mark's wife had given me. It's only a small book so it's easy to carry and it doesn't get bogged down with listing everything, just the most common birds. We drove back in the morning, and Susan made some joke about it being a good job my mum was a dyke. But mum didn't laugh.

I pass the binoculars to Becky and point to where the nuthatch is. She watches it prod at some bark with its long sturdy bill, then it gives a quick twit, twit, twit, twe-twe, before flying to a neighbouring trunk.

—It's a nuthatch, I say. —Have you seen one before?

—No.

—Nice, aren't they?

She nods. I think she's not as mad with me now. Perhaps she wasn't mad. Sometimes people are quiet because they are in a quiet mood, or because they are enjoying the scenery. It is nice scenery, it's certainly better than Weaste or Ordsall, it's even better than Buile Hill Park.

Ashley stands up, —I've got an idea.

—What is it? I say.

—Wait here, Ashley says. —I'll be back in a bit. And he strides off, fists rammed into his pockets, towards the shack. His sudden movement has scared the nuthatch off. They're quite a shy bird really. Hang on, I think, I better go with him.

My mum went a bit funny after that operation. She and Susan split up. My mum came back from the shops one day and heard some banging in the bedroom. She found Susan in bed with this woman she worked with. So that was that. Mum would be really quiet for weeks, and then she'd go out to this pub in town near Chorlton Street bus station and sometimes she wouldn't come back in the evenings. This would go on for a few weeks and then she'd say she wasn't drinking again. She'd take us out shopping and buy us things. I managed to get a lot of my books that way. My sister was into clothes and also Pulp, so she was happy to shop at Topshop or HMV. Pulp split up soon after that and then she got into Nirvana. But Kurt Cobain had been dead for about six years at this stage, so I couldn't see the point.

I could see the point of Kurt Cobain shooting himself though. I think if I had to live with Courtney Love, I would have shot myself too, so you can't blame him for that. It was when she got into Nirvana that my sister started cutting herself. One of the good things about my mum and Susan splitting up was that I managed to amass a very fine collection of ornithological books. For a while I didn't have to take them out of the library, which saved me a lot of time and effort, although obviously not money. One of the advantages of taking books out of the library is that it doesn't cost you anything. Unless you get caught. Touch wood, I've never been caught.

We find a length of fencing with barbed wire along it. We find some dead beetles impaled along the barbs and Becky wants to know why they are there. I explain that they will have been put there by a shrike. They do that. Once they have had their fill, if food is plentiful, they continue to catch it, only they impale it on spikes, thorns or barbs – a sort of larder.

It's a funny thing with birds, they are always on the brink of starvation. That's one of the problems with flight – weight. They have to be the lightest they can be at all times, so they can only ever eat enough to immediately sustain them. A bit like a jockey. They can't ever really satisfy their appetites. We talk about shrikes, the red-backed I saw earlier, the lesser grey, the great grey and the wood chat shrike. The masked shrike is still on my list, waiting to be ticked off, but not the red-backed anymore.

—We'll have to get fixed up with something soon, Becky says.

—How do you mean?

—Somewhere to stay. I've got money, she says.

He's been a long time, I'm thinking and I'm wondering what his idea is. I suppose you've got to let him give it a go. I'm not too hopeful though. We examine the edges of the copse. We find a pellet, too small to be anything other than a hawk or a falcon. All I can think about though is ravens. The barrenness of the landscape should provide lots of dead carcasses. Sheep sometimes lose their footing in this terrain and can fall and break their legs. The only non-human enemy the raven has to face is the golden eagle, as they compete for food. But we're unlikely to find any round here. Remains of ravens have been found in eagle pellets, according to the book, but they could have been taken as carrion.

—According to the book, there's a well-established crag-nest somewhere near here, I say, examining the maps at the back.

Becky has the binoculars now and scans the horizon. —There's some sticks gathered, looks like it could be a nest, she says.

—What's that there?

But it's just rooks. —It'll be dark soon. We can't stay here much longer. Becky sits down on a rock.

—Come on, let's try round the other side of this crag. But she wants to have a rest. She takes out the bread, meat and cheese and we eat. She takes out some chocolate and she hands me a chunk. I bite it in two and chew. It is soft with the heat and soon turns to mush in my mouth, like an over-sweet cloying paste, all wet and claggy. It's hard to know what the appeal is.

I realise that Ashley has probably gone to talk the man round. I doubt it will work though. He won't want to stay in a B and B, but I don't let on to Becky, perhaps we can sleep in the car.

—You know we're going to find you. It's Dave's voice. I don't say anything, just swill the chocolate mush around my mouth, avoiding swallowing it. —It was a mistake leaving the car near the shack. You should dump it somewhere, he says. —By the way, you're right about The Met, it would look great if they filmed it round here. The car chases would look ace round some of these bends.

I don't say anything.

—Are you alright? Becky says.

I must look worried because she seems concerned. Eventually I have to swallow the claggy paste. —Fine.

—You seem a bit distant.

—Me? No, why should I be?

—I'm enjoying myself, she says. —It's funny, when you live here you take it all for granted. You look at all the tourists and wonder what all the fuss is about. Then, every now and again, you see it like they do. Mum's from Suffolk, it's really flat down there. Have you been?

—What's that?

—All this, she says, and she waves her arms. She means the countryside. —Mum says we don't know how lucky we are. It's all flat farmer's fields down there and pink houses.

I've read about that. The farmers have got rid of a lot of the hedgerows in order to make more arable land and this has led to the decline of whitethroats, linnets and yellowhammers.

—They look really sweet, she says. —Pink houses. But mum says they're pink because the farmers mix pig's blood with whitewash.

—Doesn't it smell?

She shrugs. We wouldn't waste good pig's blood in Salford, we'd make it into black puddings. We sit in silence. I take out my book and flick through it. I can feel Becky's eyes watching me.

—Let's try something.

—What?

I lie down. Becky lies down too. She wants to know what we are doing. I explain that it's an old trick. You play dead and it attracts the ravens. We lie there for a while, looking up at the sky, at the dramatic change of cloud formations. And it makes me think, it is just drops of water and yet it feels so substantial. I get kind of giddy watching the cloud formations change. Becky is cold and gets to her feet. I get up too.

Eagles and ravens are enemies although they prefer to live by a sort of truce most of the time. We see lots of rooks and carrion crow. We see a pair of goshawks, which isn't bad going. But we don't see Ashley traipsing across the moors. We don't see Ashley at all. I'm thinking about what Dave has said, about

85

the car, and about him and his mates finding us. But it wasn't as though they saw us leave Kendal, so there's no reason they would head out for Helvellyn.

One thing worries me about Dave, Ashley told me he had a radio device that picked up the police radio band – a scanner. If the car we stole has been reported, it's likely that a call was put out to the police in the area, with a description of the car. Is it possible that Dave picked it up? I suppose it is. But it's unlikely and I should try and stop myself from having these thoughts, they are not helping at all. Think about ravens, not Dave. They breed early and fly in flock displays around seven or eight in the evening around this time of year, according to the book. The ravens pair for life and make very loyal spouses and good parents, but if one of the old birds is shot or dies there is no nonsense about going into mourning. The survivor goes out and gets a mate straight away. I like this mix of practicality and loyalty.

I leave Becky watching for ravens. I head back to the shack. When I reach the shack I find Ashley standing some distance away in a clearing. He is throwing his knife at a tree trunk. I need to talk to him about what Dave has said. Ashley throws his knife, it hits the trunk but it doesn't stick in and he walks over to recover it. He walks back to his spot.

As I approach Ashley he looks over to me, but there's no real expression and I can't read from it whether he's been successful or not.

—Alright? I say.

He ignores me while he concentrates and throws the knife. It hits the trunk again, but it doesn't stick in. I try again, —any luck?

He shrugs. He goes over to his knife and picks it up.

—We didn't find any.

—Eh?

—Ravens.

—So.

He goes back to his spot.

—I've just heard from Dave. I wait for a response, but I don't get one. —I think we need to dump the car.

—Fuck that.

Ashley throws the knife. It doesn't stick in.

—I'll do it if you like, I say. Not that I've ever dumped a car for that matter, but how hard can it be, you just find somewhere out on the moors and set it on fire. No, that's probably not a good idea. A fire would attract attention. I could find a lake maybe, get out of the car and push it into the water. We are in the Lake District after all. I bet if you dredged these lakes there'd be hundreds of dumped cars at the bottom.

—What the fuck you doing with Becky?

—She's one of us, I say.

—Bollocks. She's just interfering. She's got nothing to do with what we're doing.

—She wants to find ravens too.

Ashley goes to the tree and picks up the knife. —Fuck ravens. We were alright on our own, he says. —Just the two of us running away from Dave. He goes back to his throwing position.

—What's wrong?

—Nothing's wrong.

—Yeah there is.

Ashley throws the knife. It hits the tree but it doesn't stick in.

—Ok, I'll tell you what's wrong. Becky is what's wrong. Sticking her nose in.

He goes to the tree and picks up his knife. He goes back to his throwing position. Becky is approaching now, behind Ashley. He doesn't see her.

—She's just some daft bitch you want to fuck. And I'm supposed to think that's ok. Fuck her. Fuck you.

He throws the knife. It sticks in.

—You think she's going to stay with you? Posh birds like that, they don't want people like us.

I go to say something to Ashley but he walks off. He walks towards the shack.

—Where you going?

—Where do you think?

I pick up pace in order to keep up with him.

—How you going to convince that man to let us stay?

Ashley pulls out the bag of skunk and waves it in front of my face. He takes half of it and puts it into its own bag. He stashes the other half and keeps this half in his fist.

—But how do you know it's going to work?

—I don't.

—What you going to say?

—I'm not.

—What?

—You are.

He takes my hand and opens it out. He places the bag of skunk on my palm and folds my fingers around it. —Listen, if it doesn't work so what, you've not lost anything. Say it's just for tonight. I'll wait here. He stands by a tree and pushes me towards the shack.

I traipse back to where I've left Becky. Ashley refuses to move from his spot. He's becoming a pain now. I walk over to where she is standing.

—You were a long time, she says.

I go over to her and put my arm around her. We watch as dusk gathers behind the crags and the rooks travel over our heads. The sky is pink and grey and yellow and the clouds are low.

—I've got a surprise, I say.

Larks

Among their own tribe, ravens almost always have the company of their smaller companions. So it's good that we are seeing lots of carrion crows and rooks. Ravens will attack them if their nesting sites are too close and there is a bit of competition for food, but other than that they seem to get on. The kettle boils and Becky mashes up the tea. She brings two mugs over, one for me and one for her. Ashley and the man are outside, sharing a spliff and watching the sun set.

He is called Smiler. It turns out he's got a soft spot for skunk and it's been a long time since he's had any. Becky hands me a mug. The door of the pot-bellied stove is open and we stare into the flames as they darken the edges of the chunks of roughly chopped wood.

—I've got a text from my dad, Becky says.

I don't say anything, just carry on staring into the flames.

—He wants to know if I'm coping alright on my own.

—What you going to say?

Ashley walks back into the room.

—It's not a good signal in here, she says, —I'll text him back.

I nod to Ashley, —Alright?

—Yeah.

—Wanna sit down?

—Nah, I'm alright.

He goes to the fire and pokes it with a stick. Sparks fly.

—I made you a cuppa, I say. I get up and hand him mine. Becky's busy texting. Ashley takes a sip from the chipped mug then hands it back.

—So what do you want to do?

—Go somewhere else.

—Well, look, we can do. I just want to have a go at finding the ravens. After all, that's why we're here.

—What are you talking about?

He seems to have forgotten that's the reason we're in Helvellyn, because it's good raven country.

—I don't give a flying fuck about ravens, he says.

—We're going to have another look for them tomorrow, but tonight, you decide what we do. Ashley stares into the flames now. —Listen, anything you want, tonight's your night.

Ashley is in the back, me and Becky are in the front. I'm in the driver's seat and Becky is in the passenger's. It's dark outside, but we've got the light on inside. We sorted things out with Smiler and he's gone for a walk to the pub, about three miles down the road. Ashley wants to go for a drive, but the arrangement is that we find a good place to dump the car after.

—First things first, Ashley says.

I reach into my pocket and take out his stash. I sift through it and find a paper wrap.

—Is this it? I say. He takes it out and has a look.

—That's the stuff, he says, and passes it back.

I reach over for a road atlas and open up the parcel. It contains a white-grey powder.

—I'll have first shufty, he says.

It's ketamine. None of us have ever had it before but in the spirit of adventure Ashley suggested we try it. Becky is up for it, but wonders what the effects are. There's only one way of finding that out, I told her. I use Ashley's knife to chop up the lines. As I chop I can feel apprehension build in my stomach. I'm not sure about this, but I don't want Becky to pick up on my mood so I don't let on. I don't tell her it was Ashley's suggestion.

—Don't skimp on those lines, he says.

I look down at the lines I'm cutting, they look like fat lines to me but it's too late now to back out. It's quite crunchy and the blade keeps getting encrusted with ketamine crystals. I try and chop it as fine as I can.

—Aren't we better doing a small line first. See how we come up?

Ashley shrugs. —Nah. In for a penny.

Becky gives me a look of apprehension and bites her bottom lip. I take her hand and give it a squeeze.

—It'll be ok, I say.

The lines are ready. I take out a ten pound note and roll it up. Ashley has the first line. I take the atlas and the note and hoover up the line. It feels harsh, like snorting broken glass, not that I've ever snorted broken glass. I pass the atlas and the note to Becky. She hesitates. I nod to urge her on. She snorts her line and winces. I look around for any change. I hold on to Becky's hand harder.

—It's not working, Ashley says. —Let's do another line.

—Hang on. Give it a minute to work.

We sit in silence. We stare at each other. We stare out of the window. I hold on harder to Becky's hand. —Can you feel anything? I ask her. She shakes her head. She looks nervous.

—I'm having another, Ashley says.

He grabs the road atlas and the ketamine. He is about to chop another line but stops in his tracks. —Hang on, he says. He stares out of the window. He looks confused. And then there's a general sense of awe and confusion. It's like my mind is watching my body and watching everything else but is separate from it. My body feels mostly numb. Words form in my head but when I go to say them I can't make the right noises.

We sit, I don't know how long, it might be two minutes or two hours, wide-eyed in wonder at colour and fabric and shape. The shape between things. The pattern on the car seats. I'm aware of Becky. She looks confused. I want to comfort her, but I don't know what that means any more. The word 'you' forms in my mind and looks for another word to join onto. And there it is, moving sluggishly over the horizon, the word 'alright' with a question mark. If I could just bring those two words together I could ask Becky if she was alright. I nudge the 'you' up the hill, but it rolls back down again. With great effort, I crawl towards 'alright'. I try and edge it nearer to 'you', but the work is slow.

I stare at Ashley. He looks like a cartoon character. Is he a cartoon character? Perhaps he is. A Warner Bros cartoon not a Disney cartoon. Perhaps we are all in a cartoon and someone is drawing us. Dave. Dave is drawing us. Why did you think that? Where is he? He must be near to us. Don't think about Dave. Think about anything other than Dave. Dave wants to kill us. Dave is going to kill us. Stop it. Stop thinking about Dave. Stop thinking about death. Dave. Death. Grass. Think about grass. Cool, wet grass. Flowers, the sun, a great crested sunset.

So dark outside. The windows reflect the inside. The outside feels more solid than the inside. The inside is the outside. Is Becky alright? She is staring at the ground. Wish I could talk. I can think but I can't talk. She is sitting here. How near is she? Is she a very long way away or near by? I don't know, she could be both. Dave is going to kill us. Does Ashley know? He must. Why don't we talk about it? Because we can't talk. Taken too much ketamine. Trapped inside my own skull. Going round and round in circles. Unable to communicate with the world, except to blink maybe. Like Stephen Hawking. But he doesn't have to struggle to put 'you' with 'alright'. He can just do it. But he's not on ketamine. Everything makes sense if you let it come together. That's it. Don't force it. Let 'you' just drift towards 'alright'. The landscape is changing. 'Alright' is sliding down the hill. Because it's heavier than 'you'. Sliding towards it. Gravity. Thank god for gravity.

I look at Becky again. Another cartoon character. She looks waxy. There is no subtlety or shade. Just an outline and a general impression. A mask. But she is my girlfriend. What does that mean? Focus on 'you' and 'alright'. They are coming together. Almost there now. Then, as if by a miracle, I say it, —you alright?

She looks at me. Does she understand the question? Should I say it again? But it took so long to say it the first time. Don't want to start that again. Just leave it.

—Fuck.

Ashley said, 'fuck'. Was he answering my question or just saying it anyway? Fuck. Could mean 'fuck' or it could mean 'fuck'. He is fucked. We are fucked. Maybe he has been trying to say 'fuck' for as long as I've been trying to say, 'you alright?' and it was just a coincidence. They both came out more or less the same time.

We stare at things again. We do this for a long time.

—Let's... Go. Ashley says.

—Go?

—Yeah.

—Go?

I stare at Ashley.

—Out. Ashley says.

—Out.

I don't know how long this goes on. I'm aware that Ashley is trying to open the door. I see him with the door handle. He touches it. He strokes it. Eventually he pulls it open. Why does he want to go outside? It is dark out there and cold. We can stay in the car. It is like opening a fridge door. I watch him try and move out of the car. Eventually he falls head first out of the car. I see him get up and cling to the door.

—Come on.

Ashley is saying, 'come on'. I look at Becky. She looks at me. He wants us to come with him. Maybe we should go. We try and open the door. Becky can't open the door. I reach over. I manage to open the door. Somehow we get out of the car. I don't know how long it takes us but it seems to take forever. Ashley is still clinging to the door. We are hanging half out and half in the car. There is a man. Smiler. He is walking towards us.

—What's going on?

We look at him. He looks so big and heavy, like he has been made out of bricks and boulders and rocks. We stare at him. Ashley says, —on.

I say, —going.

We stare at Smiler again.

—What have you taken? He says.

—You... Taken. Ashley says.

We stare at him. He seems irritated by us.

Somehow Smiler has brought us back into the shack. I feel like a puppy saved from drowning. It is like we were all puppies in a bag thrown into a stream and now Smiler has come along and pulled us out. Cold and close to death. We are sitting at the table. Me and Becky. We both have a cup of tea. We've come round now but I still feel a bit dislocated. I hand Becky her mug and she holds it for comfort.

—You ok?

She looks traumatised. Like she has been in a car accident. I reach over and hold her hand. —I don't feel too bad now. I say to her. I'm so glad the drug has worn off. Becky nods her head.

—Why do people do it?

—I've no idea.

Ashley is outside with Smiler, smoking a joint. Becky takes a sip from her tea.

—I'm not doing that again.

—Me neither.

We sit in silence and drink our tea. The door opens and Ashley walks across. He sits down at the table.

—Well, what did he say?

Seems like Smiler was annoyed at us taking ketamine and getting so wasted but only because we hadn't invited him. It is still alright for us to stay the night. Ashley had to give him some more of the skunk. It feels good to be sitting near a fire with a mug of tea in my hand. I must focus on the ravens. All the rest is a distraction. Ravens are highly intelligent. It would never occur to a raven to snort ketamine and sit in a car for two hours. Ravens are transgressive in other ways though and this is maybe why they have fallen out of favour. Are ravens thieves? Well they probably wouldn't see it that way, but their particular brand of opportunism certainly blurs the line. I put my arm around Becky and give her a hug. She feels soft and warm.

Smiler is sitting beside the stove smoking a roll up. He smokes roll ups inside but spliffs outside. He says it's to do with his chest. When he smokes he coughs, sometimes this hacking goes on for as long as a minute until he works up some phlegm, which he shifts around his teeth and gums like a lozenge before spitting it into the belly of the stove or swallowing it back. I'm sorting out mugs for more tea. The kettle whistles. Smiler takes a towel and wraps his hand, takes hold of the kettle. It looks like a toy in his massive fist. I've calmed down now and so has Becky. The effects of the drug have completely worn off but some of the trauma attaches itself, in the same way as a shadow attaches itself – hardly noticed, behind you.

—Out the road, Smiler says to me, as he takes the kettle over to the mugs. I move out of the way and Smiler pours the water into the mugs. —I've done everything in my time, but horse tranquiliser... He smiles to himself.

He mashes the tea and throws the bags into the fire. He hands out the mugs.

—How long you been here then? I say as Smiler sits down with his tea and a fag.

—Getting on ten years now.

—No way!

—What's so weird about that? Smiler re-lights his roll up. He takes a drag and coughs. He smacks his chest with his fist and the coughing rattles then stops.

I pass Becky her tea and take a sip from my own. Me, Becky and Ashley sit around the table. Smiler sits in his rocking chair. —So what you doing here? he says.

I look over to Ashley, Ashley shrugs. —Nothing, I say.

—You've come a long way to do nowt.

Ashley looks over to me, wondering whether we should tell Smiler the truth. It would probably be ok. It might even help. But then I think, better be cautious until we get to know him. I shake my head.

—We're on holiday. I say.

—What's that, a breaking and entering holiday? Smiler says.

He eyes us up. He holds the tobacco up to me and Becky and nods.

—Thanks, I say, and he throws me the packet. I roll me and Becky a cigarette.

—So why you really here?

—It's like he says.

—Bollocks.

—We're looking for ravens, Becky says.

Smiler is a little taken aback by this, but seems to believe it. —Old King Crow, eh.

It's funny him calling them that. That's one of their folk names. They are also sometimes referred to as Odin's bird or Odin's companion. I ask Smiler if he's seen any. He tells me that there are a few round here. There were a lot more but it seems that the farmers have shot most of them. He tells me that if we hang around long enough, we'll see some. He rocks in his chair, drinks his tea and smokes his cigarette. He weighs the three of us up again.

—So you've come all this way to see King Crow eh?

Me and Becky nod. I look over to Ashley. Ashley just shrugs. Smiler must have noticed the bloodstained sports sock strapped around Ashley's right hand. He must be wondering to himself, how he did that, he's not daft. Ashley can tell him it was an accident but will Smiler believe him? I doubt it. He'll weigh it up, he'll narrow his eyes at him and the narrowing eyes will be like a fist squeezing a sponge – the truth will seep out of his pores.

We sit in silence some more. According to the book, the ravens will be busy feeding their young at this time of year. The earlier broods should take to the wing before the end of April, but the majority fly in May. It would be great to see a young raven's first flight, but I don't think we'll get chance to see that. It will just be nice to see the adults in the wild. The young adults, who are too young for parenting, should be pretty active on the social scene.

—So what's your story? Becky asks Smiler eventually.

—It's a long one.

—Why do you stay here? Why don't you live in the town?

Smiler sucks in his cheeks then spits out some loose strands of tobacco. —Don't like people. The further away I am from them, the better I feel.

None of us respond to this. I'm wondering whether we count as one of those people, or whether we are different. I suppose we must be different or else he wouldn't have agreed to let us stay.

—I did a thirteen-year stretch. I was nearly fifty when I came out. He re-lights his roll up from the flames. —I wanted to go straight, but couldn't get a job.

—What you do thirteen years for?

—Armed robbery.

—That's a long time to be locked up, I say. Just to say something.

—You get used to it. I've been in and out all my life.

—Is it not so bad then?

—It's a state of mind. You against them. First time you go in, you find the biggest bloke in the place and knock him out. It's ok after that. It was easy for me. He throws his butt into the fire and stares into the flames.

—Why's that then? Becky says.

—Street fighting. Bare knuckle. Started when I was fourteen. My mum kicked me out. I was living in Blackburn. I was born there.

He lifts up his trouser leg to reveal a football sock.

—Blackburn Rovers. The golden era. Ronnie Clayton, Matt Woods... The legendary Tommy Briggs. I still remember that header against Charlton just before Christmas 1957. I was nine years old. We beat Everton, Liverpool... We were unstoppable. Five nil against Bristol. Wembley for the FA cup final against Wolves in 1960.

He stares into the flames again, as though the flames were illuminating that period from his childhood. —I went down to London. In them days, that's what you thought. London, jobs.

—And could you make any money out of it?

—I was in a pub in Bethnal Green. It kicked off. I came out of it without a scratch. Bloke came up to me after, bought me a pint. He said 'Can you do that again?' Told me to meet him there the next night. He lined me up with a fight. Thirty quid. That was a lot of money in them days – a week's wage. I messed the bloke up pretty bad.

I look at his hands. His knuckles have been smashed so many times that they have grown back like swollen lumps. There are scars across his shaven head, where no hair grows, and most obviously the scars either side of his face.

—Did you make much money then?

—The ones doing the promoting, they're the ones making money. Took me a long time to figure that out. That's when I moved into organised crime. That's where the real money is.

—What did you do?

—I got in with the Krays.

The Yeoman Warder at the Tower of London mentioned them being locked up there.

—You didn't mess with them. But if you were handy, they could always find something for you to do. It's just how it went on then.

—Were you rich?

—I had money to burn. Cars, casinos, rings that big. He holds out his thumb and index finger to indicate. —The best things. Women. Fuck me, there were some women back then.

He stares into the flames again, lost to his thoughts. I look over to Ashley – he's hanging on to Smiler's every word. I've never seen him show so much interest in what someone was saying. He is leaning over the table, towards Smiler. Smiler comes out of his trance and addresses me. —Listen, you want to go to the top, there's only one way.

I don't want to go to the top, I'm thinking, it's Ashley that wants to go to the top, I just want to find some ravens and be with Becky. —What's that then?

—Fear. You've got to be the most feared. He stares into the flames once more. I think I see sadness in his eyes, but perhaps it's just the light. —I carry the mark of Cain, he says.

—What's that then?

—I killed a man. With my bare hands. He holds his hands out, offering his cracked and calloused palms towards us. His skin has the texture of tarmac. He seems lost to us again.

—And do you know what?

—What?

—I enjoyed it.

Ashley smiles. He seems impressed by this. Becky gives me a look: is this man for real? I shrug. I feel nervous around this man, whether what he is saying is true or not. Smiler gets up.

—That fire needs more wood. Smiler picks up an axe from the wood box. —You'll have to sleep on the floor. There's some blankets in there. He kicks a box next to his mattress. He points to me. —You chop some wood. Then at Becky, —You peel them spuds. Time for supper. Ashley gets up. Smiler wants him to go with him.

Ashley looks over to me. I'm not sure about this but don't say anything. Smiler hands me the axe and leads Ashley out of the door. Becky waits until they have gone then she turns to me.

—Where do you think he's going?

I don't know, but I tell Becky I'm off to chop wood. Outside I go to where the logs are, take one to the chopping block, but as I do, something is drawing me in the direction of Smiler and

Ashley. I can hear Smiler's heavy clomping footsteps diminish. The branches form a spiral disappearing into blackness where he has gone. The branches are encrusted with silver moss. I approach them. The dark hole in the centre of the branches is like a black surface, like the film on a stagnant pond. I reach out my hand and immerse the fingers into the darkness.

Then I am on the other side, following them, I'll see what this Smiler wants with Ashley. I head in the direction they went, careful how I walk so I don't make any noise. I walk so softly I am almost floating on the surface of the forest. I'm not sure my idea was a good idea, it's cold and dark outside and I don't think Smiler will be too pleased if he catches me following them. At the very least we'll be without a roof for the night, at worst.......

Blackness. The cool air prickles my skin, I don't have a torch but my eyes soon adjust and the light from the window casts a pale grey rectangle onto the ground. I listen to Smiler's feet tramp the earth. I wait until they fade, then go towards more darkness.

Vultures

We were in the car. Me and my sister. In the back of the car. Mum had a job then. Not for long. I was six, maybe seven. Mum was driving back from the weekly shop. I was looking out of the window. On one side, the road – the hypnotic slash of traffic. Reds, blues, speed smudging the colour. There was something violent about it, better to let the lines slip and blur.

On the other side, the verge. Then there was a bird, a kestrel, hovering above the road. It was the first time I'd really noticed a kestrel hover. Like it was painted on the sky. Like it was part of the sky. Everything else was moving and there was just this kestrel acting as a fixed point. The whole world blurring and swirling but the bird was indifferent to it. The wind was making the branches of the trees sway and the telegraph wire wobble, but the kestrel was as still as a photograph.

We'd both broken up from school. We'd started hanging out in this wood. It wasn't really a wood just a wild patch of land where the old railway track dissolved into the industrial estate. But to us it seemed magical. There were trees – sycamores mostly – and big bushes. There were flowers too, bluebells. We'd collect them for mum, put them in a milk bottle, try and cheer her up. It seems daft now but this boy called Phillip Murphy said it was haunted by woodland spirits and I believed him. I don't think my sister did. But I'd told her I'd seen them. I hadn't but I had convinced myself I had, so that it didn't feel like lying. I convinced myself I'd seen strange shapes mutate from branches. That I'd seen creatures creep from the base of old trees.

The car came to a halt. I looked up. We were home. It had been maybe three years since dad left but I could still feel his absence. Not the same place. And mum – she had changed. She didn't seem to have any time any more.

We helped mum get the stuff out of the boot. Helped her put it all away in the kitchen. There wasn't much room and we had to pile stuff on top of stuff while mum sorted out the fridge. Things were going off. Rotting carrots and sour milk. Mum was in a foul mood. She'd had a problem at the checkout. The card she was using hadn't worked. The man on the till had handed it back. She had to go through her purse but didn't have enough notes to cover it. She had to go through it all – put some of it back. There was a big box of wine I'd suggested she put back. Mum snapped at me, she gave me a crack round the head. It wasn't a hard crack but I cried anyway. She didn't put the wine box back, she put back soap, shampoo and make-up. Other people waiting behind us were getting frustrated. They kept giving mum dirty looks. But when they looked down at me and my sister they smiled at us.

Mum was rushing around shouting at me and my sister for letting the milk go off. Why hadn't we drunk it? We were wasters. So many people dying in Africa of starvation. There were yoghurts also past their best and she was getting annoyed about that, about how ungrateful we were. I didn't dare tell mum that I'd gone off them weeks ago. I'd been throwing them in the bin – hiding them under other rubbish. It was easier that way. Only, I'd forgotten this time. I said that it was dad that used to drink all the milk, not us. This seemed to make her more annoyed. I got another crack. I cried again. She was ramming veg into the salad box. There was too much of it to fit, but she wouldn't give up. She was forcing it in and then the side of the box split and she swore.

I was trying to reach up with the eggs but mum knocked me with her elbow and they fell. The yolks broke, began to seep from underneath the cardboard – the whites and yellows stretching across the lino. Mum went down on her hands and knees. Picked up the box. It dripped with egg gloop. She held it in one hand and stared at it. Her eyes were fixed on some point in the distance. Time stopped for a moment, then more gloop dripped out and it started up again. Her hand went limp and the box smashed back onto the floor, splashing the egg slime further across the surface. We were all sobbing now. The splash of tears joining the spilt yolks.

Then I was at the door, signalling my sister to join me. She did. We made our way up to the woods, leaving mum crying, on all fours. I thought it best to not be there when mum was upset, it only seemed to make her worse.

We'd come out without our coats, but it didn't matter. We made our way along the road, cutting across the field towards the old railway track. There were some brambles and I got a stick and cleared a path, thrashing the stick, liking the sound it made as it whipped the air. It was nice having my sister follow me. We didn't really play together. There was an abandoned hut I'd found some time ago. I think it was an old chicken coop. We'd been there a few times. It still had a roof and you could play games in it. You could even stand on the roof.

Before we even reached it, though, I could smell smoke and then I could see smoke in the distance. As we approached the hut we could see a man huddled over a small fire. I remember being annoyed about this. After all, I'd discovered the hut. It was mine. I moved towards the man, brandishing my stick.

—What you doing in our hut? I said to him.

The man seemed startled, but then he smiled.

—This isn't yours.

—What are you doing here?

—Warming my hands.

He was too. His hands were huge, the knuckles like skulls. There was thick dark hair growing from his fingers. I moved closer.

—How did you make that fire?

The man smiled at me.

—That's a secret.

—We've got a secret. He didn't say anything so I said, —If you tell us how you made that fire, we'll tell you our secret.

I was sitting next to the man now, looking him up and down. My sister sat next to me. It was a neat little fire. I liked the way the twigs were arranged. But there were no matches to light it. The man had a stack of twigs he was adding to the fire bit by bit.

—You tell me your secret first. I'll have to decide if it's worthy of my fire.

I looked over at my sister and she shrugged. —I've seen creatures in these woods. Little men and women that came out of the trees when I was hiding from them.

The man nodded and smiled to himself. He looked at my sister, —Have you seen them?

—Not yet, but I don't come to the woods as much as him.

Then I had a thought. —Are you one of them? I said to the man.

The man laughed, but then he went serious. He looked at my sister and then at me. He stared deep into my eyes. —Yes, I am. I'm an ogre.

I thought about this. He was a big fat man with an overcoat. He wore boots and his hands were thick and coarse. He had a beard and a hat. He had a strange smell. He could be.

—You're not an ogre, I said at last. —Ogres live under bridges.

The man laughed again. —Who told you that load of old nonsense? Of course we don't, we live where we want.

Then I had another thought. —But don't ogres eat children?

The words came out before I meant to say them. I was scared now, but the man just chuckled.

—Of course not. Is that what your mammy tells you? It's something that parents say to keep you away from us.

—Why would they want to do that unless you were bad?

—It's because they don't know what they're talking about. Only children can see us, and that makes adults suspicious. If there was an adult here now, they would think you were talking to yourselves.

I remember being comforted by this. —So are ogres friendly then?

—Oh yes. You have nothing to fear from an ogre.

—Where do ogres live then? Where do you come from? my sister said, but I don't think she believed he was an ogre.

—We live in the woods, but we can go anywhere we want. Most of the time we're invisible you see. You two caught me by surprise, I didn't get chance to make myself see-through like I normally do.

I imagined him fading so that he was like the raw egg whites.

—Of course, it wouldn't have mattered if you'd been adults.

—So do you know the little men and women I saw then?

—Oh yes, elves, gnomes, fairies. We're all friends. We help the trees to grow you see. The gnomes work the soil and look after the roots. The fairies tend to the birds and the buds, the leaves and the insects...

—What do you do then? My sister asked him, still not convinced.

—I tramp the earth down. Any trees that are too old or are dead and I bring them down, so their branches can go back into the soil.

I remembered how we left mum crying in the kitchen on all fours, and I suppose it must have occurred to my sister because she nudged me and said we'd better be getting back.

As we walked off, I turned to the man. —Will you be here tomorrow? I asked.

—Yes, but you won't see me.

—Is there any way that we can get you to be seen again?

—Yes, you can bring me some food and some beer.

—Do ogres drink beer then?

—Oh yes, it's an ogre's favourite drink is beer.

We always had plenty of beer in the fridge, and wine, and spirits.

—We'll come back tomorrow with some food and beer then, I said.

—Good kids. You do that for me. You might have to think about me really hard to get me to appear.

The eggs were still on the floor. The fridge door was half open, the fridge had turned itself on and was humming. The stuff that hadn't been put away was on the work surface. We crept into the living room. Mum was sitting down with a large glass of wine, staring out of the window. My sister was clutching a bunch of bluebells, but she knew it was the wrong time. We went back into the kitchen and finished putting stuff away. I loaded up the fridge and my sister got a cloth and wiped up the mess. After I'd got ready for bed that night, I went to my sister's room in my pyjamas.

—Shall we go to the woods tomorrow?

She was reading a magazine, but she looked up and nodded.

We went back to the abandoned hut the next day. The fire was a few charred twigs and ash. There was no ogre. I took off my rucksack and unloaded it. We had a four pack of lager, cheese sandwiches and crisps. We laid them out for the ogre.

I opened one of the packets and offered it to my sister.

—Do you think he'll come?

She took a handful of crisps, but she didn't say anything. After a while, I opened one of the cans. It was the first time I'd drank lager. I didn't like it. I passed it to my sister, but she didn't like it either. We ended up pouring it away.

We didn't really play together after that, me and my sister. I wasn't bothered. I was happy on my own most of the time. Shortly after, we moved. My sister got in with a new crowd who used to hang around near the shops. We moved from the estate where I'd grown up to Ordsall and to the flats. I didn't mind so much, I liked being high up. There were house martins and swallows and swifts up there. And there were rooks. By the side of the flats there was a park lined with trees and in those trees were rooks. They'd wake you up in the morning and at night they would roost in flocks and they made you feel like you were part of them. I never felt alone as long as I could hear the rooks.

Funny thinking that bit of scrap land with a few trees was a wood. This is a wood, and it's dark and the trees go on for miles. I'm trying to walk without breaking branches. It's hard. I have to stand well back of Ashley and Smiler and only walk when they walk. They keep stopping to re-light their roll-ups, or get their bearings. I don't know where Smiler is taking them. They make their way through bracken, clearing my path. Smiler has a torch and a stick to thrash the undergrowth.

—It's just through here. Smiler says.

Ashley says something but I don't hear what. They walk on again in silence.

—You're on the run aren't you? Smiler says.

—No.

—You can't kid a kidder.

I don't catch what Ashley says and they walk on again in silence.

—I've seen it. I've been hunted and I've been the hunter. I know the look... This way, he says.

They veer to the left and come to a clearing. Smiler shines his torch around then he gives it to Ashley to hold. He tells Ashley to point it at something then he moves some bracken to reveal a wire snare with a rabbit caught in it. The rabbit is still alive and it thrashes about. Smiler chuckles, —What did I tell yer?

He takes the rabbit and hands it to Ashley. They swap the torch over and Ashley holds the rabbit but it flaps about. —Remember what I told yer. Grip it by its neck. Ashley does.

—Now take its head, and give it a good hard twist. Like you're taking the lid off a jam jar.

We do and I hear the neck snap. Smiler pats Ashley on the back. —You know, being tough, it's not the same thing as being cruel. He takes the rabbit off us and removes the snare. Then he takes a knife and he starts to skin it. —You do what you have to do, he says. —You don't do any more. Sometimes what you have to do is go as far as you have to go.

We hold the torch on the rabbit as Smiler guts it. —You want to be top dog right?

—Yeah.

—Well that means you've got to go further than anyone else is prepared to go. But you've got to remember, once you're at the top, look out for the ones underneath, cos they're watching, waiting for their chance.

I decide this is a good time to head back and creep through the cleared path. Once I'm a good distance I make a run for it until I see the light from the shack in the distance. Becky is peeling potatoes over the sink. She seems relieved to see me. She gives me a big smile. She puts the potato she is holding in the pan.

—You ok?

—Yeah, how you getting on?

She's peeled quite a few potatoes. I've no wood to bring in though. She takes another potato and starts to peel it.

—There's something quite pleasing about peeling a potato, she says.

I'm glad I've not had to use my axe, that Smiler was just taking Ashley to check out his snares. There's nothing wrong with finding a rabbit and teaching Ashley how to prepare it for cooking. I think that's probably a good lesson for Ashley. I don't think he's done much food preparation. Perhaps Smiler is ok, but I'm going to keep the axe close by just in case. After all, there's not just me and Ashley to think of, I've got to look after Becky too. If the world ever runs out of food, like burgers and chips, there will always be plenty of rabbits. But then we'd be competing with the raptors again, and the government would put a price on their heads, like the king did in the old days.

—Do you think he's telling the truth? she says. —About prison and street fighting?

A curl of peel shaped like a hook hangs from her knife and then drops into the sink.

—I know one thing.

—What's that?

—He didn't get that scar shaving.

She peels in silence for a while. I watch her work the skin from the potatoes. I take Ashley's knife and go over to the sink. I take a potato and start to peel it. There's not much room and I have to hunch forward. The lump of potato feels nice in my hand, just the right size for my fist to grip round. I know what Becky means, it feels sort of natural. My right leg and hip are pressed against Becky's left leg and hip, and the warmth from her body starts to warm me.

—We should go, she says.

—Where?

—I'm not sure it's safe here.

I weigh this up in my mind. Where is safe? At least here there are three of us against one. There are no guns. But she's right, we can't stay here for long, apart from anything else, I don't want to. Smiler makes me feel uncomfortable, and I'm aware of the effect he is having on Ashley. It's like we have split into two groups.

—Thought you wanted to have some fun, I say.

—Well, yeah, but...

—How about if we stay the night, I say. —We can get up early in the morning and look for the ravens.

She doesn't answer, just peels the potatoes.

—What do you think?

She shrugs. I don't know where we are going to go from here. All I know is that I want to go wherever Becky goes. I'm not convinced we can find the ravens, but for the first time, it doesn't really seem to matter.

Eventually she says, —How important is it?

And I know straight away what she means. She's talking about the ravens. I tell her about my list. I go over to my book and show her.

—There are 189 birds on there now, I say.

She scans the list and laughs. —That seems a lot.

—It is.

She scans the list again in more detail this time. —I've never even heard of half these birds.

She passes me the book and I put it back. She puts her arms around me and kisses me.

—You're a bit of a weirdo really aren't you?

I don't mind being teased by her. If you get picked on for using big words, you stop using them, but it doesn't stop you thinking them. And if you get picked on for being into birds, it doesn't stop you being into them, in fact, you get more into them, but you just keep it from them. I actually feel less attached to the list than I ever have in my life.

Still, part of me is still driven by it, it's a funny thing I suppose, and I'm surprised Becky doesn't find it weirder than she does, I don't normally share it with anyone. Thinking about it now, I don't think there's anyone else I've ever told about my list. It's always been my secret. Now someone else knows, it doesn't seem as important. There's that need there though, underneath, almost like an itch, and it would be satisfying to tick the raven off at last. More than that, it would be really satisfying to finally see them in the wild. Even more than that would be to finally see them in the wild with Becky. I suppose that's it.

I start to tell her about vultures to take our minds off things. Vultures remind me of ravens. They're both scavengers feeding off carcasses of dead animals. They also remind me a bit of Smiler. I think it's the bald head. Like ravens, they rarely attack a healthy animal but may kill a wounded or sick beast. They are a very valuable bird because they can eat diseased flesh containing anthrax and cholera bacteria.

The thing is though, they're becoming endangered, particularly in India, where farmers routinely medicate their animals with a pain killing drug which keeps the animals working for longer but which kills the vultures. This has led to hygiene problems in India as dead animals now tend to rot or are eaten by rats or wild dogs. India now has one of the highest incidences of rabies.

The Parsi people of India, who are basically Zoroastrians, have a tradition which involves the vulture.

—What are Zoroastrians? Becky says.

I don't really know. I tell her about the tradition. When a Parsi dies he or she is taken to the Tower of Silence where the corpses would normally be eaten quickly by vultures. This is because they believe that earth, fire and water are sacred elements and shouldn't be contaminated by the dead.

—That's daft, she says.

—Well, yeah, but the thing is, because of the decline in the vulture, lots of dead Parsis are taking too long to decompose and they are trying to save the vulture. Parsi communities in England want to introduce the vulture so that they can dispose of their dead according to custom.

—That's not going to happen, is it? she says.

I tell her about the Jews in Broughton and that wire going round Northumberland Street, twelve foot up in the air to ward off evil spirits.

—Isn't there any trouble? she says.

—Not when I was there, anyway. Now, don't get me wrong, It would be great to have vultures in England, but my fear is that they would be competing with the raven, and the raven, being the smaller of the two, might lose out. Eventually the vulture would wipe out the raven, a bit like the story with the grey and red squirrel.

—Right, she says.

—The Parsi community should encourage ravens to eat the dead. Build the Tower of Silence and surround it by ravens. It's a brilliant solution.

—Mmnn, she says, and laughs. She thinks I'm joking.

—Apparently Freddy Mercury was a Parsi, I say, as the door swings open and in walks Smiler and Ashley, with Smiler holding a dead rabbit by its back legs.

—What's that you say? Smiler asks.

—We were talking about Parsis. Freddy Mercury, he was a Parsi, I say.

—I've heard it called lots of things in the past, but I've never heard it called that before, says Smiler, and they both laugh. I don't think Ashley knows who Freddy Mercury was.

Storks

It was shortly after the trip to Scotland. Mum had split up with Sarah and she had developed this thing with the taps. She had this thing about polishing the taps and if she saw a fingerprint on the taps she would grab your hand and try and match it up. Sometimes she wouldn't talk for days, you'd talk to her but it was like you weren't in the room. Then one day she took a knife to my sister. My sister was winding her up saying there was too much butter on the bread. Next thing she had the bread knife at her throat. I tried to calm her down, but she didn't seem to hear me. Her eyes were wild and she was shouting, in my sister's face.

There was an incident with a neighbour too over the bins. A few nights later I heard all this commotion. I got out of bed. The door was open and they were dragging her down the corridor. I woke my sister and we both ran downstairs. We watched as they bundled her into a van. They wouldn't let us go with her. They took us somewhere else.

We had to stay at this place for a few weeks. It wasn't very nice. When we went back to the flat with mum, she was speaking to us again. She was sorry, that's what she told us. There'd been some mix up with the medication, she said. It wasn't her fault. She bought us both an ice cream and we watched television together. It was Carry On Up the Khyber. We all laughed when it was revealed that Private Widdle was wearing underpants, but only after mum laughed. Mum laughed and then I looked at my sister and we knew it was ok to laugh, because sometimes you would laugh and mum would cry. Like that time when we watched this comedy sketch show. There was this man who owned a mansion and he was in love with his gardener but he

113

couldn't tell him and we thought it was funny, but mum cried about that.

We had a Hawaiian pizza from Dial-a-Pizza. Perhaps a week later the nightmares about storks began. They're very striking, particularly the marabou stork. The word marabou comes from an old Arabic word meaning the tomb of a holy man. I'd only ever seen them on the telly and once in real life when we went to a bird sanctuary in Yorkshire. It's sometimes called the undertaker bird because from behind, with its cloak-like wings and back and skinny legs, that's what it looks like.

Like ravens and vultures, the marabou stork is a scavenger, so its bare head is well adapted. A feathered head easily gets clotted with blood and bits of spleen. Not ideal when you keep sticking your head in a corpse, I suppose. In the nightmare the birds would always be there. Usually in number. I'd be walking to school for example, and I'd spot one by the bus stop staring at me, then I'd see a line of them queuing for the bus. Or they'd be gathering around the all-weather pitch at break time. Staring at me. It got so I couldn't sleep at night. In the end, the only way I could stop the birds from appearing in my dreams was to draw them. I'd do pencil drawings of them hanging from trees by their feet. Or pictures with their heads impaled on the school railings – hundreds of stork heads – one on each spike. I'd spend hours doing these drawings but it worked, the storks stopped coming. It was always marabou storks though, never any other type.

Smiler is dishing out the rabbit stew onto enamel plates.

—Get that down yer neck, he says, as he hands us the plates. He gets bottles of beer and opens them with his teeth. He hands them out. He takes his own food and beer and sits in his rocking chair. We're sitting round the table. He starts to eat. We all start to eat. It doesn't taste bad. There are too many potatoes maybe, but we got a bit carried away.

—You didn't finish your story.

—Did I not?

Smiler's been telling us about some of his robberies, from a long time ago. I was interested at first until I started thinking about storks.

—Well, you see, I became the bloke who did the nitro, he continues. —I had the steadiest hands in the game, he says, and he holds one of his hands out to demonstrate and I'm struck again by the knuckles, like boulders, like skulls. Becky gives me a look: here we bloody go again she seems to be saying and I smile at her. It's the longest I've ever been with a girl, not counting mum or my sister and I don't feel uncomfortable at all.

—It was one of them big chest safes. You can't rush a job like that. Forty minutes, an hour. If it doesn't work, you go home empty handed. If you get disturbed half way through, you scram. So Barry passes me the nitro and I get to work. I'd been at it for about twenty minutes tops, when I get this tap on my shoulder. Thinking it's Barry, I turn around. It's not Barry. Barry's done a bunk.

—Who was it? I say, not really caring one way or the other, but I can see that Ashley is hanging on to every word. Since I've been with Becky, I've started seeing Ashley in a different light. He doesn't seem to me now to be a raven, not even a crow, more of a jackdaw. He seems to have physically shrunk and his hair doesn't seem as shiny.

—What we call the long arm of the law. In this case, Mr Security guard.

—What did you do?

—Calm as you like, I stood up and said, 'What seems to be the problem, officer?' He was so taken aback that in the moment it took him to register, I gave him the Smiler head butt.

He puts his bottle of beer on the floor and his plate too and demonstrates.

—Right between the eyes. You should have seen it, fell down like a dead man.

Ashley laughs. Then Smiler notices me and Becky giving each other a look and he turns to me. —What's the matter with you? he says and I join in with the laugh. I give Becky a look too and she joins in, although my laugh and Becky's laugh don't sound genuine.

Smiler guzzles his beer. —Don't you look at me like that, he says.

He stares at me and I say, —I... I was miles away. I was thinking about the ravens. We're going to look for them first thing. Where should we look?

He thinks about this. —There's a few nests around here, he says. —There's a crag not too far away, I'll show you in the morning. There'd be more if it wasn't for the farmers. Can't blame them, he says. I want to tell him that the farmers only shoot them because they think they kill their lambs, but they don't. A raven only eats dead things. It's not a killer. That's why they keep out of the way of the farmers. The raven is a very clever bird. But I don't tell him this, I just nod and smile at him uneasily. He stands up and empties the bottle.

More bottles appear and we neck these. Then he gets out the whisky. He passes the bottle around and we all have a few swigs of this and he starts telling us more stories about his criminal past, which Ashley seems pleased about if no one else. The bottle goes round again, more stories. Another swig of the whisky. Things get a bit hazy. Becky gives my thigh a squeeze and winks at me. I feel all warm and glowing.

Smiler is getting worked up about something. He's shouting now, —You think I'm stupid? You think I'm thick? I'll show you, you bastard!

I don't know what he is talking about. Ashley just watches him, not sure how to react, but he isn't shouting at Ashley, he isn't even looking at Ashley, he's shouting at some imagined person, someone from his past maybe, someone from when he was inside.

Now he's on his feet again. He positions himself in a spot, steps around it, defining it. He rolls his shoulders and hunches them up. He bunches his fists and draws them up to his chest, then up to his face, so that his deep-set eyes peer over his knuckles. He bares his teeth and growls. He starts to shadow box. I want to laugh, but I stifle it. As he carries on with this shadow boxing, he starts to make pained noises. It's as though there really is someone in the room fighting with him.

He works himself into a frenzy, like he's not going to win, which is funny because there's no one there, but none of us laugh. He's struggling, he staggers backwards, almost loses his footing. He bumps into his rocking chair, then the side of the table. He rights himself and raises himself up to his full height. His eyes have gone wild and he roars. Becky squeezes my thigh again, this time not out of affection, but out of concern. Ashley's had another spliff and he's not really taking it in. I give Becky one of those looks that acknowledges that this bloke is crazy without making too much of it, but I'm not really sure he even knows we are in the room.

Then he seems to get the upper hand. He gets the man on the floor and he's stamping on his head. He drops to his knees. He's talking to the man now, whispering in his ear. We just sit and say nothing. We try not to watch him and focus on something in the distance. Becky puts her head against me and pretends to be asleep. I think this is a good idea. I put my head on hers and close my eyes. I can hear Smiler whispering to this bloke, then he's mumbling to himself, I can't really make out what he says.

That night, for the first time in many years, I have a nightmare about the marabou storks. I'm back at Becky's place, only in the living room is a stork, perched on the back of the sofa. It's staring at me. I walk into the kitchen and there's a stork on the fridge by the door. Another stork is perched on the top of one of the large paintings. It shits and the grey mix of urine and excrement drips down the canvas. Then I hear the front door open and I look through a gap in the kitchen door. It's Dave with some other blokes. They walk into the living area and then the dining area. I see Dave go upstairs. I hear him search the rooms. Then a stork flies down the stairs with Ashley's blazer in its beak. It drops to the floor and one of the men picks it up and sees the Roseway badge on the breast pocket. He nods to himself and then shouts up the stairs for Dave.

When I wake up I know that Dave and his gang are coming for us.

Woodcocks

A greenfinch, a pair of wood pigeons, a skylark, six lapwings, a golden plover, a stonechat, three magpies, god knows how many gulls, jackdaws, rooks, crows, but no ravens.

I was up first thing, before anyone else. I had a walk round some of the surrounding woodland. Everything was so still. The sun was just a sliver of light edging the horizon. I was in a strange mood, half-awake, the world of dreams draped over me like a shadow. It was like I was watching myself from the trees, a bird's eye view of the world, a bird's eye view of me, scurrying about, thrashing ferns with a stick, prodding at the undergrowth, picking up clumps of earth, breaking it up with my fingers, sniffing it. Clambering on all fours. Trying to be an animal, sharpening my senses to all that is alive and to all that is dead and rotting.

When I went back to the shack everyone was still sleeping. I crept into the space I had left next to Becky, still smelling of the earth. Still feeling that dream-like feeling. When animals dream their eyes flick and jerk like ours, their limbs thrash about and they grunt or make whatever noises they would when going about their waking routine. Do they make a distinction between the two worlds or is it all one to them? Perhaps in order to find ravens I must become more like a raven.

We crouch in the undergrowth near to the crag that a rather hung-over Smiler pointed out to us this morning. No one mentions the incident. I don't think Smiler even remembers. Ashley is with us, I have Becky's binoculars and I'm looking at a clump of trees, when I hear Ashley receive a text. He takes his phone out and opens the text. I see his face go white and I'm about to ask him what the matter is, when I see it, a woodcock.

I can't be sure at first. I think it's a snipe but I focus and see that it is plumper than a snipe and its bill, although long and tapering, is thicker than a snipe's. As I watch it walking through the undergrowth, it sort of bobs its bulky frame along, almost like it's doing the conga. It's brilliantly camouflaged against woodland but here in the open it's easy to spot. Its black eyes and black bar on its head and neck contrast with its dead leaf colour. I nudge Becky and pass her the binoculars.

I take out my field guide and turn to the checklist. I scan the list. No, according to the checklist I've never seen a woodcock in the wild. I take out my pen and tick it off. Brilliant. That makes 190 species in the bag. Apart from killing a man and one or two other hiccups, this has been a really valuable trip. Besides, I didn't really kill a man, Ashley didn't really kill a man either, it was the car. No, not even really the car, seems unfair to blame the car. The killer of Dave's brother, if indeed he is dead, was the concrete. It was the concrete that killed Andy.

I leave Becky watching the woodcock and crawl through the undergrowth towards Ashley. I ask him what the matter is but he just ignores me. I ask him again and this time he takes out his phone and shows me the text: *I no where U R. U killed my brother now its your turn.* I look at Ashley and he stares back at me. There is only darkness in his eyes. I pass the phone back and he puts it away. Becky comes over and wants to know what's wrong. I give Ashley a look and he shakes his head. She sees that we are both upset and she puts her arm around me. Ashley watches her jealously, I think. He stares at me with hate in his eyes. Becky is picking all this up.

—What's wrong?

He gives me a look and then turns to her. —This is boring. That's what's wrong.

I look at Becky and shrug.

—It's your fault, he says to Becky and points. I just look at Becky and give a slight shake of my head. —We were having a laugh. We both ignore him. I wonder about this. Were we having a laugh before Becky turned up? It was certainly very exciting, I don't think I've ever had so much excitement, but not exactly a laugh, no, I wouldn't use that word. He picks up a stick he has been using to thrash the undergrowth and hits the ground with it. —Slag, he says, under his breath.

I don't even think about it. I just go for him, —You what? I say, as I grab hold of him. He has the stick in his hand and he swings it round. It whacks me in the back of the head and I fall to the ground. Becky just stands there watching me fall. I come round and she is standing over me.

—What happened there? she says and shakes her head. Ashley holds the stick as though he is about to whack her with it.

—I'll kill yer, I'll kill both of yers. He stares at us both with rage in his eyes, then he screams out and runs off.

I get to my feet. Becky looks shocked. Then she turns to me, —You alright? I feel the side of my head. There's blood on my hand. Becky examines it. There's not too much blood.

—You took me by surprise, she says, —I didn't expect that. We sit down on some rocks. My head throbs from the whack and a numb ache starts to form. I use the sleeve of my jacket to halt the flow of blood. It isn't a bad cut. She says I should be more careful. I wonder whether I should go after him, but it's too late, he's already run off through the woods along with the woodcock. The woodcock is a shy bird and is easily disturbed. I think maybe that's why it has evaded me for so long.

After the shock has worn off, Becky wants to know what's going on. It feels weird keeping things from her, and although I know Ashley wouldn't want her to know about the text, I can't help it, it all comes pouring out. I tell her everything I know about Dave and about what's happened so far.

—Hang on, she says, —not so fast. Who's this Ashley?

121

But Ashley has run off so I can't show her Ashley. —He was my friend, I say.

—And he's not now?

—I don't know.

—I still don't get it, you were running away from someone called Dave? Why? I thought you came here to find ravens?

It's confusing for her, I know, there's a lot to take in, but I tell her what I think, that Dave has come to the Lakes, that he will have gone to Kendal, that he will have found Becky's house.

—Calm down, she says, and takes my hand in hers. —Think about it rationally. All what you've said, doesn't make sense. This Dave, I mean, why would he be here? He will have gone back to Salford... Don't you think?

I nod my head, trying to believe this to be the case, but perhaps I'm less than convincing because she persists.

—Look Paul, even if he did make it to Kendal, even if he did find my house, how would he know we were here, hiding out in a shack in Helvellyn with some nutter who drinks too much and fights imaginary blokes?

She laughs, and I join in. Of course she is right. It feels good to laugh and it sort of lightens the weight I've been carrying around.

—What was that all about? I say, and she knows I'm talking about last night, and she shrugs and we laugh again.

Then after some time she says, —Do you really think he's dead?

I think about this, there's no point in denying it. —I don't know for sure, but he really took a smash. We'd picked up a lot of speed and he went right up in the air and landed on his back real hard. If he's not dead, he'll be in a hospital bed somewhere strapped up with tubes and wires and all that.

—But you weren't driving the car?

—No.

She thinks about this. —So where's Ashley now?

I shrug, he's run off. I'm not his keeper, I don't know where he is all the time. And then she does something quite strange, she smiles, and I'm taken aback by this. How is that something to smile about? We watch the clouds form into clumps as they drift over the horizon. We watch their shadows darken the fells, like damp stains, then lift again. That's something that you miss when you look at a photograph, the constant change of light and shade. It's the same with people, that's why people sometimes look quite strange in photographs. I think about my photograph with dad, his arm round me, smiling, but what do I really know about him? Do I even remember him, or do I just think I do from that one image? We look happy, smiling at the camera, but doesn't everyone do that?

We've moved around a lot, it's got to be said, but if he'd really wanted to find me, wouldn't he be able to? It's not as if we've left the country, we've not even moved out of Salford. Well there was that time we lived in a Maisonette in Miles Platting but apart from that, it's been mostly Salford: Weaste, Ordsall, Higher Broughton. How many schools are there? How long would it take to go to them one by one? A couple of weeks? Then I start to feel the weight again, and that hollow in my stomach and I try not to think about it. I look back at Becky and she is staring at me.

—You'll be alright, she says, and she gives my hand a squeeze. There's a chill as a cloud darkens the area where we are sitting, and I suddenly feel very alone. In a strange way, thinking about Dave is a lighter thought than some of the other thoughts I'm inclined to have, if I don't watch myself and I tell her about my fears. Well, I tell her what my main fear is.

—Ashley said that Dave had this device in his car.

—What do you mean?

—He's got a scanner. She nods her head, she knows what they are. —That car I stole near your house, it would have been reported to the police and a call would have gone out. Isn't it possible that Dave has found the car where we abandoned it?

Again, she thinks it over. —Ok, it's possible, but it's pretty unlikely... Don't you think?

I wish I could believe it. I wish we hadn't been so stupid as to dump it so close to the shack. She laughs it off. —Don't be daft, she says.

Of course she's right, but I'm still not convinced. I tell her about my nightmare and about the storks.

—What are you now? Telepathic? Or maybe you can see into the future?

Again, I can't fault her logic. I'm not telepathic and as far as I know, I can't see into the future. We talk for a long time about what we should do next. We need to move on, if only to ease our minds. Whether Dave is a real threat I don't know.

—You really are a strange one, she says. But again, she's just teasing me, she's not being mean. I decide not to tell her I can fly. It's not the right time, she has enough to deal with.

—My mum and dad, they're coming back soon. I have to go back to Kendal.

They've been texting her again.

—I can't go back there, I say. —They'll find us. We need to move on... Stay.

—I can't.

—Just till your parents get back... Please.

She stares at the ground for a long time.

—I'll stay until we find the ravens, she says at last.

I put my arm round her. I hold her. I don't want to let go. She knows how much the ravens mean to me. And I can't stand the thought of her going back to Kendal. So I agree. I want to find the ravens, and I also want to stay with Becky. But then what happens when we find the ravens? I lose Becky.

We spend another few hours on the moors: curlews, grouse, more jackdaws. We keep thinking we see ravens, but they turn out to be crows or rooks, so hard to tell without a sense of scale, you need perspective, and in any case, I'm quite unsure about finding them now. It was easy in the Tower of London when they were standing next to a packet of crisps or a coke can say, but here it is much harder. It's mid-afternoon when we make our way back through the woods towards the shack.

We hear a commotion, a harsh chorus of football rattles. Then we see magpies fly up, still making their clacking cackle. As we do we come across a nest of squirrels that has fallen to the ground. As we approach it, we see that the squirrels, only a few days old, have provided the birds with a feast. Their guts are exposed and their heads ripped open. One of them has had its head ripped off its body and there is just a bloody hole there instead of a head. Only a few days old and bald, they look like human babies.

Accentors

Foxes, badgers, crows, ravens – it seems farmers don't like any of them. There is no doubt about it though, that the raven is being held back not just by farmers, but game keepers, park rangers, the Forestry Commission, local councils, the government, tourists, egg collectors, hikers, mountain climbers, grouse hunters, clay pigeon enthusiasts, quarry workers, hang-gliders, para-gliders, other types of sporting knobheads, and knobheads in general with shotguns who just like 'shooting things'. I've noticed that a lot of the new forests round here are plantations of conifers. The problem with this is that they are grown too close together. They don't allow ground vegetation. There's no way that a bird as big as a raven can use most of the forests round here to hunt. You might as well build a retail park.

We make our way through such a wood. Trees planted so close together that all you get on the forest floor is pine needles. What use is that to anyone? We don't talk, just wend our way through the darkness. Spruce, I ask you, since when did we demand for our countryside to be populated by Christmas trees? I don't even like Christmas trees at Christmas, so why would I want them growing out of the ground? I'll say this for mum, she's never bothered with that stupid tradition. About a week before Christmas, she'll get a box out from under the bed, with a few baubles, tinsel, stuff like that. It gives the same general impression.

Apparently the first word I said was 'bap bap'. Not mum or dad but bap bap. We were in Albert Park in Broughton, according to mum. Dad was still with us. I must have been one and a bit. We were feeding some ducks, me and my sister, and that's when I said 'bap bap'. Not quack quack, but pretty close. After that, I called all birds bap baps. Until I got to about four. This is all according to my mum. I never called them birds. I learned each of their names: sparrow, magpie, pigeon, starling... Learned all the names of them before I used the word 'bird'.

When persecuted, ravens are shy and wary birds. You can't blame them for this, in fact it seems like a healthy attitude. I'm quite a private person myself. I'm thinking about this as I walk behind Becky. It's the first time I've opened up to someone who's not my mum. The behaviour officers at school used to try and get me to open up but it never worked and I just went more into myself. Nice people, a lot of them, but do-gooders. My mum calls them nosey interfering fuckers, which I think is a bit harsh. But not as harsh as what she calls social workers. Or doctors.

In intelligence tests ravens score better than wolves and dogs but not as well as monkeys or dolphins. But I'm not sure tests really work. I'm in the bottom groups for both Maths and English, but that's because I never go to class. One teacher actually refused to mark my English work. She said I hadn't done what I was asked. But technically we were 'told' to do it, not 'asked' so she was wrong about that as well. I don't think she understood what I was writing about. The truth is, most teachers aren't very bright and don't like very bright kids – it shows them up.

I've seen this a lot now. The kids who do really well at school are those who want to please the teacher. It means something to them. They are like dogs that will keep bringing the stick back as long as you give them a stroke. There's a story Ratcliffe tells about some red grouse researchers. Apparently they started marking the nests with sticks but had to stop because pretty soon the ravens realised what they were up to and started to feast on the nests.

For some reason ravens collect golf balls. Perhaps they like the look of them. They can't be collecting them to play golf and they have no value to the bird at all as far as I can make out. I don't know why they do it. I like to think that the real reason is to annoy golfers. I used to do the same thing myself. I'd actually run on to the putting green and nab the balls. The nearer they were to the hole, the more fun. You can always outrun a golfer.

As we approach the shack, Becky stops and turns. She grabs my hand and kisses me.

—We'll give it one last go tomorrow.

—Yeah.

We walk on in silence for a while, the shack now visible.

—What we gonna do about Dave?

—Stop worrying about him, she says.

I put my arm around Becky. We haven't made love since that time in her bedroom and I'm eager to do it again. But we're too close to the shack now. I should have tried it on before, up on the moors, but the whole thing with Ashley distracted me. And the squirrels.

When we get to the shack, there's no sign of Smiler or Ashley. Smiler's left about eight or nine empty beer bottles near his rocking chair but that's the only sign he's been here.

—No one home. Becky says. She walks over to the stove.
—Fire's still going. Let's make something to eat.

I look around the kitchen area. I find the pan of stew from last night. There's quite a bit left, should be ok if we heat it up. I put the pan on top of the stove. Becky fills the kettle. She puts it on the stove next to the pan. She takes two mugs and swills them out in the sink. She finds some teabags and puts one in each mug. She puts the mugs down on the table. She sits down. I take some wood from the pile in the basket and throw it into the belly of the stove. I sit down next to her.

The kettle boils, I mash up the tea. We eat the stew, drink the tea. I wash up the bowls and the mugs. We've left enough stew for Ashley and Smiler. We sit and chat and laugh, but all the time I'm getting this growing sense of unease. He's been gone four hours now.

—How's your head?

I lean over and she has a look at the cut. She tells me it's not so bad. It's stopped throbbing now. Something's not right. I can't put my finger on it, but something feels wrong. We chat some more, although not about tomorrow, I'm trying not to think of Becky leaving, I'm trying not to think about that. Suddenly, in walks Ashley.

He looks at both of us, but I can't read his look. He walks across the room then sits in Smiler's seat. He stares at the flames. Becky gives me a look, what's the matter? I shrug. Eventually I say, —You shouldn't have done that. He doesn't respond, just stares deeper into the flickering flames.

—Who are you talking to? she says.

There's this silence which seems to build up, like it's getting heavier, until I say,

—Where's Smiler?

Still staring into the flames, Ashley says —He went out.

—Has he eaten?

—He's gone into town. Meeting a mate. Said he was going to eat in the pub.

Becky gives me a look, then says, —Are you alright, Paul?

—Well he has, right. Since when were you an expert on Smiler? For the first time since he walked in, Ashley turns round to look at us. Then he turns back to the fire. I look over to Becky and shrug. The silence builds again, until I say —We left some stew for you. It's still hot.

—Not hungry, he says, not looking up. Eventually he says, —I'm off first thing in the morning.

—Good, I'm glad. Why don't you go now? I say.

—I'll go when I want.

—So what's keeping you?

—What the fuck's it got to do with you? Why don't you and that fat slag there keep your noses out? He stands in the shadow so I can't see his eyes. —Are you gonna come or not?

The truth is I don't want to go anywhere with him now. Whatever it was I saw in him has gone, and yet I feel responsible for him somehow. I want to go with Becky. I've tried to persuade her to come with us but she rightly pointed out that her parents will call the police if she doesn't go home, and we'll be in even more trouble. Can we be in even more trouble? I suppose it is possible. I can't think straight. We can't go to Kendal, in case Dave is there and we can't go back to Salford. Where can we go? Ashley gets up and takes the axe out of the basket. He goes outside.

I look over to Becky who's giving me a strange look.

—Seriously Paul, are you sure you're alright?

I manage to smile. She puts the palm of her hand on my forehead.

—You've not got a temperature.

We sit in silence for a bit. Then she says, —I got a text off my mum, I'm going to have to go first thing.

—You can't just abandon me.

—I'm not abandoning you Paul. This has been fun, but-

—But what? It's over, is that what you're saying?

Becky shakes her head. She's not convinced, I can see that. She gets up and looks out of the window watching Ashley chop wood. I don't know why he's chopping wood, there's plenty in the basket. All around, dusk. The gradual dimming of the light. I stand next to her and watch Ashley chop.

—I don't want you to go home, I finally manage to say. —Come with me.

—Why don't you come with me? she says. —You'll be safe there.

In the distance I can hear the rooks' roosting calls, although the usually soothing sound of their 'kaw kawing' today sounds harsh and unwelcoming. As it builds I can feel it digging and digging into the back of my head.

Owls

I can't get to sleep. I'm thinking about storks again. I know if I close my eyes I will see them and I will see Dave. How close is Dave to us now? If he has found the car, he could be wandering these moors right this moment. I try not to think about it. Block it out. Smiler hasn't come back. It's late. Maybe there's been a lock-in down the pub, or maybe he got so drunk he fell asleep on a park bench or under a bush. I'm on the floor with Becky under thick musty blankets. I can feel the warmth of her body next to me, my hand on her tummy, I can feel it rise and fall like bellows.

I was reading about a study which was carried out in Scotland by some society or other and it recommended reintro-ducing wolves to Scotland. It's been over two hundred years since the wolf roamed the moors of Scotland, before they were hunted into extinction. It was something to do with solving the problem of deer numbers. You need about five hundred wolves apparently to bring the population of deer down to a desirable amount. I can't see farmers going for it though, or ramblers for that matter, but I bet the ravens would like it. For once they wouldn't be the only outcasts, and they would also benefit by being able to feast on the deer carcasses once the wolves had had their fill.

Surely the main problem though would be sheep. Why chase a perfectly fit deer when you can easily outrun a sheep and get just as good a meat? That would be the wolf's logic. And I bet that's why they became extinct here in the first place. Besides, it seems to me there are plenty enough wolves in this world already. Right now I feel like a little pig waiting for one to come and blow this shack down. At least if Smiler was here I wouldn't feel quite so scared. Not that he could stop a bullet, but I bet he'd give one a run for its money. Would a bullet even penetrate that lumpy thick crust of skull?

Try not to think about bullets. Try not to think about wolves. Or skulls. Think about something nice. I think about Becky, her naked body. But then I think about Dave coming for Becky. I see Andy's crumpled body. I see blood. I see Dave staring back at me. I see Dave with his hands round Becky's throat. A ring ouzel. I saw one when we were in Scotland. We stayed in this farmer's cottage in Dumfries. We hired it for a week. Mum's medication had really straightened her out and, although the cottage wasn't very nice and was surrounded by about three foot of cow shit, we actually quite enjoyed it.

I went for a walk away from the farm one day. I was watching some birds by a hay storage barn. There was a wren hopping low down in the stonework, looking for spiders. There were some jays and some thrushes under some hawthorn eating some berries. From the back I thought it was a blackbird, but then it turned to face me and I saw its white breast. The first and only time I've seen a ring ouzel. Lovely that was. Then there was that time I saw a firecrest in a tree in Wales – first and only time I've seen a firecrest. So small and fidgety, but so brightly coloured.

I press the nightlight on my watch, nearly two o'clock. I'm wondering what time do they do lock-ins round here till? Who's to say, it's not as if they can get many police checking up on them. Police. Don't think about police because that will make you think of Dave. Now you're thinking of Dave again. All roads lead to Dave. Maybe not, but there was only one road leading to Kendal. He must have made it to Kendal, despite what Becky says, there's no question about it. Maybe I should ring my mum. She keeps ringing me and texting me, so it seems a bit mean not to contact her, but what's to say? Maybe I should just text her and say everything is fine. But everything isn't fine. Still, it will make you feel better and then perhaps she will stop ringing you. What if Dave is in the pub now with Smiler enjoying a pint and talking about criminal things they have done. What are you doing up here? Smiler will say, and Dave will say he is looking for us. Would Smiler dob us in? Maybe not, but what if Smiler tells Dave about us, before he knows Dave is looking for us? That's possible. Dave might say something like, so what brings you to the pub, and Smiler might say his shack has been taken over by two lads and a lass on the run.

I rub my chin with my hand and feel stubble. I've only been shaving for just over a year. I can't grow a full beard yet, just sideburns and some hair above my top lip and on my chin, but it's getting long. Need to shave it off. Becky might not fancy me with stubble. Some girls like stubble but best not take the risk. Smiler's got a razor, I've seen it by the sink. Ashley's asleep in Smiler's chair. He drank a lot of whisky and smoked himself into a stupor, crashed out really early. Didn't say hardly a word to us. Can he be that jealous?

Well, yes, I suppose is the simple answer. Maybe he's thinking about Dave as much as I'm thinking about Dave. Thing is, he's really what Dave is looking for, not me. I'm just part of the general package, not that I think that's going to save me if and when Dave catches up with us. We are both in the shit, no two ways about it. Think nice thoughts. 'If', what am I talking about 'if' for? It's 'when'. How long can we keep on going for? He's not going to stop until he's hunted us down. Nice thoughts. The twite – no that's actually a rather small dull brown bird. Not nice at all. Why did you think of a twite? Of all the birds you could picture in your head you had to picture one of the dullest.

How about a swan, a lovely swan, or one of the terns? God, there are so many terns. Why are there so many terns? You don't

133

stand a chance with terns. I've even got a poster of them on my wall to help me out. But they all look pretty much the same. Start with Arctic, nice black head, but so has the common tern and the roseate. And the gull-billed tern. Thinking about it, so does the whiskered and the little tern. They've all got black caps more or less, what are you thinking about. Forget the heads, focus on the bills. It's the bills of terns that you need to learn in order to recognise them. They're all a bit different. But, Christ, how close do you have to get to them before you can use bills for recognition?

Ok, don't think about terns, that's just winding you up, making you feel stupid, think about something more reassuring. How about owls? Christ, you love owls and you've not thought about them for ages. So I lie there in the dark, with one hand on Becky's soft tummy and one hand on my chin stubble and I picture owls in my head. Their fat heads and no neck. Their liquid amber eyes. The way they turn their head, like twisting the head on that bubble bath figure you used to have. Twist the head so it is facing the other way round. Their feathers. The barn owl with flight so soft, so silent.

The drains on the estate. The leak. It was coming through the living room ceiling, like a tap left running. And there was no dad. No dad to go up on the roof and fix it. We were telling mum to ring the council. My sister picked up the phone. She didn't know any numbers. She got through to someone. I don't know who, but this led to another call then another. The rain was pouring down and pouring through our house. Eventually, two men came from the council. One of the drains on the roof was blocked. He told us it was blocked with bones and fur and little skulls of voles and mice and shrews. A barn owl probably, was using our roof as its supper table. And my sister was shouting at mum. —It's your fault, it's your fault. It's your fault dad went. Mum wasn't doing anything, just standing there. The man looked embarrassed. He left. But my sister was still

134

screaming at mum about dad. Try not to think about dad. More owls.

The barn owl. The scops owl, snowy, eagle, little owl, pygmy, tawny, hawk, long-eared, short-eared, the lot.

The Raven

We wander across the moors. We approach a crag. I think I see a raven nest but when I look through the binoculars, it has been abandoned. Still, it shows that this is a suitable area. We carry on walking. Ashley is some way behind us. He has hardly said anything all morning. The sky is overcast, and there are dark clouds in the distance, but they look too high up to rain. The Lake District has one of the best-documented raven populations in Britain. Tree nesting is uncommon though, so we have more chance spotting a crag-nest. The rocks poke out like fractured bones, casting dramatic shadows.

The unevenness of the ground and the frequent sheer drops along the path suggest to me that this is quite treacherous walking for sheep and I imagine lots of sheep have fallen down a ravine and either died on impact or broken their legs and died of starvation later. All good carrion opportunities. There are lots of sheep about, some of them in precarious positions, perched at the edge of a drop munching away at the tough grass. We find sheep bones picked clean of the meat. We come across a whole carcass, with the head detached and lying a few feet away. It is early for lambing season but we see one or two very young lambs that can't be more than a day or two old.

We watch them as they huddle up to their mothers for protection. Their legs hardly strong enough to bear their weight. How different a lamb seems to a full-grown sheep. We see other sheep that are plump with unborn lambs and must be due to give birth any day. Lambing season is feasting season for ravens. There are many casualties, still births, fatigued mothers, weakling offspring unable to make it to their feet and always the afterbirth, the placenta, which is good nutritious food. Many ewes after giving birth are too weak to rise. Then there's foot-rot and other ailments. A harsh spring is good and will increase the casualties.

The foxes, buzzards and eagles, even red kite will be the first at the table, opening the carcass up and exposing the innards. They will eat the tastiest meat, the prime cuts, the neck, the breast, the shoulder, the leg, the scrag and flanks, leaving the less appetising entrails for ravens. Once the ravens have finished, the scraps left will be eaten by crows and maybe even magpies. The last inedible bits will provide fly maggots a start in life, and these maggots in turn will be food for other birds, and these birds will be preyed on by raptors. And so it goes on, life eating life eating life.

Like birds of prey, ravens produce a pellet of undigested material. We find a small grey bundle that could be a raven pellet. I break it up with my fingers. It disintegrates leaving a grey powder of wool and fur and bone fragments. A pellet left out in the open like this would soon break down, so this must be a fairly recent casting and could indicate that this is a favourite eating area. I'm getting excited. Perhaps the raven used the sheep's skull as a perch, keeping watch as it picked at the flesh.

The raven's powerful bill is ideally shaped for tearing at flesh. Despite the fears of many a shepherd it seems it is highly unlikely that a raven will attack a healthy ewe or ram. If the animal is sick, then it's a different matter. In which case the raven is likely to give a helping hand, driving them over a ledge to their death. Basically, speeding up the process. According to this morning's reading though, I was wrong about lambs it seems, a lamb is a different matter, and although nothing like as widespread as paranoid farmers seem to think, a raven will sometimes attack and kill a lamb. So I was wrong, ravens are killers.

Looking at the sheep around me, they seem lifeless and dull. All they do all day is chew tough tasteless grass. In a way, the raven is saving the lamb from its dreadful fate – to become a boring adult. I like lambs but by the time they get to adulthood, I've really gone off them.

One of the problems the raven has got, though, is the way it eats. It seems it has bad table manners. It will usually begin on an ailing animal by pecking out the eyes. Then the tongue. It may seem revolting but eyes are very nutritious and easy to pick out. It's also rather clever if you think about it. The action of pecking out the eyes, secures the food supply. An animal which is blinded is as good as dead. Sometimes a sheep will roll on its back and be unable to right itself. It's a bit sneaky, but it's a good opportunity to get in there and peck. Then the sheep will die and you've got your grub sorted out for the week. Maybe even two weeks. The raven has its own young to feed.

Besides, a good shepherd should be watching out for his flock, so it's really his fault. Smiler doesn't seem to like the birds. He was saying yesterday that they sometimes pinch rabbits from his traps, but rabbits are plentiful and there are enough of them for both man and bird. In any case, how does Smiler know the thief is a raven? It could just as easily be a fox. The thing about the raven is, it's not fussy. Yes, it likes a nice bit of mutton, but it also eats eggs, beetles, larvae, seeds, buds, nuts and berries. We find another pellet. I crouch down and examine it. Becky does too. Ashley is some way in the distance. I hand it to Becky. She turns it over in her hand and gives it me back.

—Are you sure that's what it is? she asks me.

I crumble it up in my palm. Amongst the grey dust, fur, bones and wool, I find a thick rubber ring.

—Look, I say, holding the ring up. She takes hold of it.

—What is it?

I explain that this is what the farmers use on lambs to remove the tails and also to castrate the males. It's a very common thing to find in a raven pellet. There are also fragments of stone and grit and I explain that the birds swallow this in order to help them digest some of the tougher food they eat. This is what I really love about Becky. I'm explaining all this but she doesn't think it makes me weird. She actually seems interested. I picture saying the same thing to mum or my sister. They would just go, urgh, that's disgusting, and pull a face. It's not disgusting, it is life. We follow the sheep-walk as it climbs up towards some impressively large crags.

Ravens can be pirates too. It's not uncommon for a raven, or more likely a pair of ravens, to rob a short-eared owl of a field vole say. I think about the ravens at the Tower, the raven master getting fresh meat from the market for them every day and yet, still, there they were, in the bins, scoffing discarded chocolate bars, chips and sandwiches. We are now close to the crag and almost in its shadow. We stop to have a look around, and as we do, I spot it. I hold the binoculars up to the dark shape in the sky. It's true at this distance it could easily be a crow, but then it does something which immediately identifies it as a raven. It rolls.

First it soars and then glides, then it draws its wings in and rolls over onto its back. It stays like this for two or three seconds, then reverses the movement by rolling back the opposite way and spreading its wings again, going back to its normal flight. The display takes my breath away. I say nothing, just watch it fly. Then it does it again, and again, each time it drops slightly, making it look like it is tumbling through the air. Becky is standing close by, I can feel her next to me and I turn to watch her stare up at the bird. I pass her the binoculars. She takes them and watches the peculiar tumbling flight display. It is almost like it is doing it again, just for her. I put my arm round her and give her a squeeze.

Then another one, its mate, appears. I watch as they silently rise together, flying into a stiff breeze. Then simultaneously, they make a headlong dive with wings almost closed. Checking the dive and catching the wind, they plane steeply upwards.

Regaining with effortless grace the height lost. They follow, in perfect unison, tumbling, twisting, diving and climbing. Now over the crag, they are joined by another pair. Without a sound, they begin a similar dance about a hundred yards away. The two pairs fly in towards each other, almost touching wings, then all four birds carry out the same acrobatics, tumbling, twisting, diving and climbing again.

The display lasts for about ten minutes then the two pairs fly off north.

—Wow, Becky says, handing me back the binoculars.

I'm still speechless. She squeezes my hand and kisses me. I think to myself that this is the most perfect moment of my life. That all my life has been working up to this moment, holding Becky, kissing Becky, on the moors of Helvellyn, watching four ravens for the first time, in the most beautiful and graceful flight display I have ever seen. I put my arms around her and pull my lips away, gasping for breath. I hold her tightly towards me, tears in my eyes and a lump like a raven's casting catching in my throat. I cling on to her, not wanting her to see my eyes. I hold her for perhaps a minute, trembling, her body next to mine.

—Come on, let's follow them, she says. Ashley is still some distance away, in the shadow of a crag. Perhaps he will see he's not wanted and wander off. We walk at a good pace in the direction the ravens went. As we go round the crag the sheep-walk dips and we start to descend the hill and we see them in the distance, soaring and spiralling. We pick up pace but walk carefully not wanting to disturb them. It looks as though they have spotted some carrion. We watch as they circle it over and over. Then one of them drops and swoops, landing on the ground. We edge towards it. It approaches a large lump of carrion. Difficult to say what it is from this distance, but it is more than likely a sheep. We get closer. It hops and flaps its wings, a good five yards or so from the carcass. Then another lands at the other side about the same distance away.

They both follow a similar ritual, flapping their wings, jumping up and down, a few feet in the air. Then strutting around, before jumping up again. One of them bows and opens its massive bill. It bobs its head about. The other one tilts its head, as though it were trying to catch what the other one had said. It stretches its neck back, its bill pointing skywards. It does this several times, before striding about, getting closer to the carcass. They are joined now by the other pair, who land either side of the two. They strut and jump about. They flap their wings. The raven that landed first gets closer to the carrion and then backs off again. We edge even closer. The carcass is in a muddy sump and is covered in filth so that it is hard to make it out. But it's a good sized sheep alright and will provide them all with food with plenty left over.

The dominant bird hops onto the fleece, jumps up and down a few times on it then flaps its wings and flies off about two or three yards away. The other birds respond by moving in closer. Then the dominant bird hops onto the fleece again. It pecks at it before perching on the head. Then it reaches into the skull and pulls out an eye, with bloody threads like wet string dangling from it. It opens its beak and swallows it down whole. Another bird hops onto the fleece and starts jumping up and down. We walk even closer to it, ever careful not to disturb the birds, but as we do, it dawns on me that the carcass is not that of a sheep, it is too big. Could it be a red deer?

We get as close as we can without alarming the birds and as we do, I realise that the carcass is that of a person. I look at Becky and can see from the shock on her face that she has realised this too. She stares at me and without saying anything we walk closer. As we get to a few yards away, the dominant bird, with the eye threads still dangling out of its mouth, flies off. The others follow. It's a man. A large man. We see his shoes caked in mud first, then his trousers and his coat, all daubed in mud. We reach the head with the missing eye. His mouth is open but there's too much mud to make out his features. As we get closer, I see Becky put her hand to her mouth, to prevent herself from vomiting. Now I feel like being sick too. The head gapes at us with one empty eye socket. The face is covered in blood and filth.

—Oh my god, she says.

I stare at the corpse, we both do, unable to say anything. We stand staring at the body in silence. Then Becky walks over to me and takes hold of my hand. She grips it tight.

—We need to report this to the police, she says.

—Yeah, right.

That's one thing we can't do and she knows it.

—Go to the police.

I shake my head.

—Please, go to the police and report it with me.

I say nothing, just stare at the corpse. Then I say, —Dave is going to catch me.

—Then go to the police before he does. It's your only choice. She squeezes my hand again. To give ourselves in to the police is to surrender to a less hungry wolf. They can protect us from Dave. And if we report this, we will be doing a good thing. It puts us in a good light. On the other hand, it may just bring a whole heap of further trouble. I don't know what to say. Ashley has caught up with us but is still lurking in the background. He stares at me and shakes his head. I'm still not really grasping all this. I keep staring at the corpse trying to register that this lump of meat is a dead man.

Then I notice his sock showing from under his trouser leg. I get up closer to it. It's a sports sock, in fact it's a Blackburn Rovers football sock.

—It's Smiler. I say, and look over to Becky. She looks back in shock. Ashley's face is just a blank.

—No. It can't be, Becky says.

I take out a rag from my pocket and go towards the head. The sight is repulsive, but I force myself to wipe off the mud from around the mouth. It's Smiler alright. The scars at either side of his mouth. No doubt in my mind now. I don't know what to do, I look at Becky but she is frozen to the spot, then I look at Ashley as I realise the truth.

—You? Becky is staring at me and shaking her head. —Oh my god. She shakes her head again.

—What? I manage finally, and point to Ashley. He says nothing but he shakes his head.

—You did it. Admit it.

There is a long pause. Eventually he says, —I did it for you.

I stare at him then look over to Becky. She is still in shock. She shakes her head with incomprehension.

—What? I say at last.

—You wanted to see them stupid birds, well you got to see them.

I just stare at Ashley, it's like I've not heard him properly and I have to repeat his words out loud until it begins to sink in.

I look at Becky, she is shaking her head. —No... No...

I go over to her. I try to comfort her, but as I go to put my arm around her, she withdraws. I try and hold her but she shakes me off. She turns away from the scene and starts to walk away back up the sheep-walk towards the large crag.

—Becky!

She speeds up, still walking away. I run after her and catch up with her. I grab her by the arm. She shakes me off again, this time with more force. —Becky, where are you going?

—Get off me.

—But where are you going?

—Away from you.

I don't understand what she means. Why does she want to get away from me?

—You're crazy.

I'm speechless, throat clogged up with emotion. I hold out my hands, pleading, but she looks at me, and this is the bit that really gets me, she's looking at me the way I looked at Ashley, with utter revulsion. Then she runs off.

I start to run after her but I trip over. I get to my feet, carry on running, this time limping, but it's too late, I can't catch up with her. I limp after her for about three hundred yards, before she disappears behind the crag. She's gone. I stop and get my breath back. I don't feel anything, just numb. I turn back to the scene. The corpse is still there. For a moment I thought I might have imagined it. And Ashley is still there. He is standing over the dead body, casting a shadow over the man's face. Above a raven pair appear. They are high up and they soar up even higher in a widening spiral. They are waiting for us to leave so that they can feast.

Leach's Petrel

When we had the flat in Ordsall, for a while my mum was on her own. Quite a long time really. There was this bloke who lived in the flat opposite. Richard, his name was. He'd trained as a chef at one point, he told me – but all he cooked now were fried egg sandwiches. I used to go round there sometimes. I didn't like the sound of them at first, but when I tried one, I was surprised to find that, with loads of red sauce on, I really liked it. Because mum was on her own, Richard thought he stood a chance. He didn't realise mum wasn't interested in men in that way, and I didn't tell him because I liked having him around. He'd ask me what mum thought of him and I'd tell him that she liked him, which wasn't really a lie.

He started to leave notes under the door. Always a folded piece of paper with mum's name on it. Just daft things really like: great film on tonight on ITV at 8pm. Or: reading a book from the library, really good. I'd sometimes add a reply at the bottom if there was space and put it under his door, you'll have to tell me about it later. Or, let me borrow it when you've finished. I didn't sign it from mum, but I could do mum's handwriting. I've been able to do mum's handwriting since we were given homework diaries in primary school. It was one of the reasons I got excluded. Actually, that time I'd written a letter explaining to the teacher that I couldn't do Games because of a medical condition. I slipped up there by not stating what it was and he rang mum up at home to ask her.

Anyway, this time I didn't sign the notes so in my mind I still wasn't lying. It wasn't my fault if my writing was like mum's and it wasn't my fault if Richard thought the notes were from mum. Mum's handwriting is small and neat but she gets half way into a word and then just sort of abandons it, so that there's just a squiggly line where the last few letters should be. I used to think Richard's handwriting was like his voice. Almost a whisper. Hardly a trace on the paper. But he was nice and I liked him. He'd let me have some of his lager. He'd pour a bit into a glass. Not enough to get me drunk though, probably no more than a quarter of a tin. He was a shy man really but I suppose he wasn't shy around me. He didn't go out much but sometimes I'd hear him leave at ten or eleven at night and not come back till the early morning.

One time when I was round there he asked me to go to the shop for him for some milk and bread. He gave me two pounds and said I could spend the change on sweets. It was raining heavily outside and as I went to the door I saw his large green anorak on the hook behind the door. I went back into the room to ask if I could borrow it but he was on the phone. He won't mind, I thought and I put the coat on. It was far too big for me. I went downstairs in the lift. My hands explored the pockets. There were some stones in one, and a knife in another. A small penknife. I reached into the inside pockets. There was a wooden handle in one. It went through the lining. There was another knife, much bigger. It slid into a leather sheath. I slipped it back into the lining of the anorak. In the top pocket was something soft – I pulled out a black Balaclava. Wearing the anorak made me feel weird, like it was putting thoughts into my head. I didn't feel myself in the coat. I bought the milk and bread and some sweets and returned the coat to its hook behind his door.

I didn't tell Richard I'd used it, there didn't seem any point. I thought there must be a good explanation for what I'd found. Perhaps he used it for fishing, and the things in his coat were used to fish. There were quite a few blokes in the flats who would go to the canal to fish. Nothing strange about that. A few weeks later I was watching the telly with mum and there was a local news story. A woman had been attacked down Black

Friars. For some reason the council had converted one of the high-rise flats into student accommodation. The woman was studying at Salford University. It was the middle set of flats, so any student walking home would have to walk through the estate.

When the students first moved into those flats they looked like students always do. Tight jeans or leggings, big daft boots, dyed hair or a daft haircut, stupid jewellery. But within about a month of them moving in all the boys had hair like Oasis or crew cuts and they wore loose-fitting jeans and trainers, T-shirts and tracksuit tops. They started wearing gold jewellery instead of silver. The girls changed too, started wearing the same sort of stuff. Dyed their hair blonde or brown instead of red or black, got rid of the big boots and started wearing shoes. A man had jumped her at about midnight when she had been walking home through the estate. She'd managed to get away and out-run him.

The telly showed a photo-fit picture, and the funny thing was, it looked a bit like Richard. About a week went by and there was another attack. This time the woman had been sexually assaulted. I asked mum what 'sexually assaulted' was and she just said it was what men did to women. It had happened the night before, again about midnight. I'd heard Richard leave about eleven. I'd fallen asleep shortly after that so I didn't know what time he got back. I got worried about it. I thought it was Richard. And because of the notes I'd sent him, Richard thought he was in with my mum. He kept talking about her, asking me where he should take her for a date. I didn't have the heart to tell him.

I kept this secret inside me. I wanted to tell mum about Richard, but was afraid she would confront him and they'd both find out about the notes. It was just after my exclusion for faking a letter from my mum so I was being cautious. I made myself a promise. If another woman was attacked and Richard was out at that time, I'd tell mum and suffer the consequences. Another few weeks went by and I was thinking that I'd got away with it, but that night on the evening news there was another woman, again a student, who had been 'sexually assaulted'. I couldn't be sure, but I thought I'd heard Richard leave late on the night before. I asked my mum if being 'sexually assaulted' hurt. She said it hurt very much. I was going to tell her, really I was, but first I thought I'd ask Richard where he'd been. Give him a chance to explain.

I went round there. He made me a fried egg sandwich with loads of red sauce. He gave me a bit of his lager. He was smoking one of his roll-ups. He wanted to know more about my mum. I was just waiting for the right moment before asking him where he'd been, when a steel ball about the size of a marble came through the window and hit the wall just behind where we were sitting. Not easy to hit a window seven floors up. Must have been a catapult. Richard grabbed hold of me and we ducked down. He crawled over to the window but the kids who had fired the shot were running off.

He asked me if I could keep a secret and I said I could – and that was true. He told me he was part of a vigilante group. I asked him what that was. He told me there was a gang of them and they were trying to drive the drug dealers out of the estate. I'd heard about this. Neighbours had spoken about it. He said that one of the drug dealers had found out about him and that's why the steel ball had been fired. It all made sense. I believed him. I could never really imagine him 'sexually assaulting' a woman even though I didn't know what that was. I'd just seen how friendly he was with mum.

The point was, I wouldn't have had him down as a vigilante either. Not that I really knew what that was, but I'd heard it involved a lot of violence. I found out later exactly what they were doing and it was pretty brutal stuff. I got told that they dragged one of the suspected drug dealers back to someone's flat and tied him to a chair. They tortured him and messed him up really bad. He had to go to hospital and have a lot of stitches. I suppose it's easy to get the wrong impression of someone.

Although I've not known Ashley long, I really thought I knew him well enough and I definitely wouldn't have put him down as a killer. I know he killed Andy's brother but that was an accident. Maybe killing Smiler was an accident. But he'd said he'd done it for me. That's what he said, so that I could see the birds, the ravens. And that's what I can't understand.

I'm driving a stolen car and Ashley has got a road atlas on his knee. We're heading towards Scotland. My idea. When we stayed in Dumfries there was no one around. You could walk for days and never see anyone. It seems like a good place to hide out. Ashley wasn't so keen, but he didn't put up much of a fight either. I don't think either of us are thinking straight. I can't get Becky out of my mind, and what sticks is the look of revulsion she gave me just before she ran off. It was like me, Ashley, Smiler, the ravens... all tarred with the same brush. Blackened by the dirt of the world. Something you don't want to even get close to, let alone touch.

I'm trying not to think about what's happened. The only way I can get the image of Smiler's mud-caked corpse or Becky's look of horror from my head is to focus on birds. Each time either of these images pops up I replace it with an image of a petrel. One of the best things about that trip to Dumfries and Galloway, after seeing the golden eagle, was seeing some storm petrels. Not much bigger than a sparrow, all black with a white rump. I saw one on its own at first. It was fluttering over the water near to where the harbour was, its wings held up in a 'v' and its feet pattering across the waves. Then I saw more. There was a trawler coming into the harbour and there were five or six in its wake. I ticked it off my list. But I've never seen the less common Leach's petrel and I'd really like to bag that one. I'd say it was a bit bigger than a storm. And the other difference is the Leach's has a forked tail.

We can lie low there for a bit, but after that, I don't know, I really don't know. Ashley has hardly said anything at all. When I came up with the Dumfries idea he just nodded. It's dusk.

I'm thinking about our next move. We've still got some money from the drugs. We could stay in a B and B. Plenty of them in Dumfries. But it might look suspicious. I'm thinking it through when Ashley says, —Andy's dead.

I don't know why he is saying this because we both know Andy is dead. It seems a strange thing to say when he hasn't really spoken for several hours. Then he says, —Dave is going to kill us. We're dead.

I think this through. Dave can only kill us if he catches us. And I'm thinking about what Becky said about going to the police. I've already spoken to Ashley about this twice but both times he just shook his head. What I need to do is convince Ashley this is the right thing to do, but if killing Smiler wasn't an accident or self-defence, it's going to be hard to convince Ashley to go to the police.

I ask him again. —Why did you do it?

—I've told you.

—Did he come at you?

I'm thinking back to the shadow boxing incident. There's no doubt about it, Smiler was a bit unhinged. I can easily imagine him getting into an argument with Ashley and them fighting. Perhaps Smiler was drunk and fell over, banged his head on the pot-bellied stove. There are lots of explanations that put Ashley in the clear.

—I did it for you.

It just doesn't make sense. He's never shown any interest in the birds at all. Come to think of it, he hasn't ever really shown any interest in me either. I'm wondering now what it was that brought us together. For me he was the cool kid and the hard kid – an object of fascination. But for him? Then I get it, he's not the cool kid at all. He's another outcast. The girls he was fooling with that day, they weren't interested in him. He needs me to feel good about himself, because I see him the way he wants to be seen. Except I don't, not any more.

It's getting dark and it's raining. I spot a police car in the rear view mirror. I don't say anything, I just sit there hoping it will go away. But it doesn't, it stays right behind us. Ashley hasn't noticed. Then its blue lights start to flash and the sirens build. Ashley looks in the mirror. I can see panic on his face. I put my foot down. The police car follows us. It gains on us. I drive off the road, the police car follows. I stop the car and we both jump out. We run through the rain across the road and into a hedgerow. Two policemen chase us but we soon outrun them.

We run past the back of houses, down narrow streets, back alleys. We stop and get our breath. We are on the outskirts of some town. We haven't gone that far from Helvellyn. According to the atlas this is probably Carlisle. We'll have to stay here for the night, go to Scotland in the morning, unless I can persuade Ashley to go to the police. If I can convince him killing Smiler was an accident, then I might be able to do that. I wait for him to get his breath, then I say, —So, what next?

We check into a B and B. We say we are eighteen. I don't think she believes us but she doesn't ask questions, just leads us to our room, at the top of the house. There's a skylight and you can see a sliver of moon refracted through the rain-spattered glass. I make us both a cup of tea. We sit on the bed in silence, drinking the tea. It's another one of those days where lots of weird things happen. Finding ravens for the first time, finding a dead body, finding out the dead body is someone we know, realising it is my best friend who has killed the man. Then losing Becky, going on the run, stealing a car, being chased by the police, finding out my best friend isn't my best friend, and now we are here in this rented attic room sitting on a bed, drinking tea.

This has stopped being fun. Every time I think of Becky I feel hollow and raw, and I can't stop thinking of her. It's nothing like The Met. For a start, it's gone on for too long. Even an extended episode would have come to the end by now. I have nothing to say to Ashley, there doesn't seem any point. I don't even want to look at him. I text Becky. I sit on the bed waiting to get a text back, but nothing. Has she received the text? Is she ignoring the text? She must think I'm like Ashley but I'm not like Ashley. I don't kill people, only by accident. I certainly don't kill people to use as bait. I'm thinking I need to get myself out of this situation and back to Becky as soon as I can. The only solution, go to the police. I could go on my own, confess to it all, but confess to what? I could say I've lost Ashley and I don't know where he is.

Who's to say anyone has found Smiler anyway. There will be hikers up there and shepherds, but it's possible no one has found him just yet. If I went to the police now and told them about Dave before they find out about Smiler then they could protect me. The truth is, I don't know what to do and I can't stand the silence anymore. The silence says I'm sharing a room with a murderer. The silence says Becky has left me. The silence is not good. I reach over to the portable telly and switch it on. I flick through the channels and see a photograph of me on the screen. There aren't many photographs of me. This is one from last year, mum was trying out the camera on her new phone. Then I think, mum must have given them the photo. Why would she do that?

Then it cuts to a news reporter and he is standing outside our school. The reporter says,

—The boy who was reported missing three days ago has been named as Paul Cooper, but they don't mention the other missing boy, they don't mention Ashley O'Keefe. My photo appears again. Three days, it feels a lot longer than that. Why did he say me and not Ashley? Perhaps it is done alphabetically. Still, I don't like going first.

—Paul Cooper is a pupil of Roseway School in Salford. He has a history of truancy and exclusion.

It cuts back to the school gates and the reporter. You can just make out the blue Care Bear on the razor wire.

—Police are wanting to question the boy in connection with the death of Brian Smith whose body was found in Helvellyn this afternoon.

Who is this Brian Smith? I wonder, then I realise, that must be Smiler.

—The boy is thought to be driving a stolen car. His description corresponds with that of a boy seen stealing a car in Kendal.

So this is why it is on the local news. BBC Cumbria or whatever it is.

—The car was found in Helvellyn last night. Police are asking witnesses to come forward with any information which may lead to his whereabouts.

I look over to Ashley. He is staring at the telly. I switch it off. —Listen, I say, —we can't stay here. If the owner has seen the news, she'll ring the police.

Ashley doesn't really seem to be taking it in. I get up. I shake Ashley. I slap him, I punch him in the face. Finally, I poke him in the eye, nothing. I go over to the skylight and open it.

We walk across the roofs of a row of terraced houses. As we do, a slate slips and falls. I peer over the edge to see if anyone has spotted it, but the street is deserted. We carry on walking. Ashley receives a text. He stops to read it. I shake him and take the phone off him. It's from Dave and it says: *I am coming.* I hand the phone back to Ashley. Dave must have seen the news too from wherever he's been staying, perhaps in a hotel in Kendal. Who knows? Still, he will go to Helvellyn rather than Carlisle so that buys us a bit of time. We get to the end of the roof. We find a drainpipe and climb down.

We walk around the streets looking for somewhere to hide out. It's still raining and quite soon we are soaked. I'm worried about my books getting wet but they are inside the lining of my coat so should be ok. Eventually we find an empty house with a 'to let' sign outside. We go round the back and peer in. It is dark. I go to the back door and, wrapping my jumper round my hand, I punch a glass panel out of the door. I reach in and release the Yale mechanism. We're in.

There's nothing downstairs, other than a fitted kitchen. We go upstairs. There's a double bed with a mattress on top. It will do for tonight.

—Listen, let's doss down here for now, I say. But Ashley is distant. He slumps in the corner of the room and builds up a spliff. He doesn't offer me any and I don't want any of it. I'm trying to think straight. If Dave goes to Helvellyn, then what next? There is nothing that connects us to Carlisle and no one who knows we went to Carlisle. Becky. He could get to Becky. I try not to think what he will do to Becky. She doesn't know where we are. I didn't say in the text, just that I was safe and missing her. Why hasn't she texted back? Maybe Dave has got to her already. I send her another text. I'm running out of credit, only enough for another couple of texts. I ask if she's alright. I wait for a reply. Nothing.

Maybe she has her phone switched off. She'll be with her parents. They will have had their evening meal, sitting in that fancy living room round that fire, talking about their holidays. Not watching television because they don't have a television. But what if they're not? What if they come home to find the house has been broken into and their daughter has gone, kidnapped by Dave. Or worse she's been sexually assaulted or butchered. Butchered. Sexually assaulted. Butchered and sexually assaulted. Sexually assaulted and butchered. Blood on the walls. Dave has written something on their living room wall with Becky's blood, and it says 'coming, ready or not'. Try not to think about that. Go to the police tomorrow. You can't be responsible for Ashley, Ashley is nothing to do with you, but what if Ashley says I did it? Who knows what Ashley will do? I lie down on the bed. Sleep. Try and get some sleep. But I can't. Thoughts are colliding in my mind. Ashley, Becky, Dave, Smiler, the police. I try and think about birds but it just doesn't work. It's the first time it's never worked and I don't know what to do without birds. They have always been there, they have always worked.

I think about all the birds of prey but their eyes all look cold and accusing, like Dave's. I try and think of other birds, but every one of them has those eyes. Then the storks appear. Every time I close my eyes, the storks are there. Becky still hasn't texted. What to do? How much credit has Ashley got on his phone? Probably not that much, but more than me. It's late. She might be in bed. I can't blame her for wanting an early night. She is probably asleep. That's why she hasn't answered her text, her phone will be switched off for the night. Stop worrying about her. But that's just it. I can't. I can't stop worrying about her. There is me, the one listening to the one worrying about her, then there is the other me, the one doing the worrying. Now I'm arguing with myself. Going round and round. Stop worrying. But I can't stop worrying. I need to know she is safe. Wait until the morning, get some sleep. But I can't sleep until I know.

Herons

A red-backed shrike, a woodcock and a raven. I was, in all honesty, hoping for a few more firsts, but the raven thing has kind of spoiled the anticipation. I'm not even looking out for anything. It's funny though, because even when I'm not looking out for anything, I can't help noticing, very high up above my head, two buzzards soaring on a thermal. They always hunt from a high vantage point. I wonder what they can see from up there. They must be able to see for miles. As far as Helvellyn, easily. I try and dismiss the thought. It's actually the commonest bird of prey in this country, although most people on the ground fail to spot them because they never look up that far.

They're a bit like an eagle really only smaller and less impressive. I watch them soar and then dramatically dive for ages, before hitting a thermal again and gently rising. They travel miles without flapping a wing. You see swifts that high up. Sometimes gulls too. Then I see a grey heron, flying low over the houses. I'm trying not to get distracted by birds. I've left Ashley sleeping on the mattress with his coat over him. I left a note saying that I've gone to get us something to eat. That it will be safer if I go on my own and to wait there until I get back.

Still no text from Becky, but several missed calls from mum and a lot of texts from her, too. I've taken a twenty out of Ashley's pocket. So I should be able to get us both breakfast and there should also be enough to get a ten-pound phone card for my phone. I'm going to ring Becky. No point keeping texting her. I buy a local newspaper. I want to know if we're in it and what it says about us. I've got my hood up so I shouldn't get any attention. There's nothing distinctive about me so it's not as though I'm easy to spot. In ornithological terms, I'm just another small dull brown bird. Of no interest to anyone really. Herons are very patient hunters and can stand dead still for long periods of time. As long as you stand still you're ok really. A fish is looking for movement, not shape or colour, just movement.

It's still early, there are not many people about. I pass a TV shop and watch. Nothing about us. One of the tellies is on the blink, not a good advert for a TV shop. You'd be better just switching it off. There's a woman with a clipboard, but she doesn't even bother approaching me and there are two fat girls stuffing sausage rolls into their mouths. I quite fancy a sausage roll. The last time I had a sausage roll was over three years ago. Christmas day 2005. Doctor Who was on the telly. It was the one where the Doctor regenerates. Rose and Mickey go shopping and are attacked by masked Santas. When they get home they find a Christmas tree, and they realise that Jackie didn't buy it.

I don't like Christmas, my birthday is quite close to Christmas, and stupidly each year, I think I might get a card or even a present for either my birthday or Christmas from dad. It's not happened yet. But there's always that chance. That particular Christmas it was my thirteenth birthday. I was hoping for snow, but all we got was drizzle.

Just me and mum. My sister was round at a friend's. There had been some words about that and she'd stormed off. Mum did ask if I wanted a turkey, but there didn't seem any point. We had the veg though, sprouts and roast potatoes. She made some gravy and we even had stuffing, but instead of turkey we had sausage rolls. Mum let me have a small glass of wine with the meal. I gulped it down and it went straight to my head. I felt like I was floating. I won a pink plastic hairslide in my cracker, my mum won a green plastic angel. We both wore our coloured tissue paper crowns and told each other jokes. I laughed. Mum quietly sighed.

I'd asked for an iPod. I got a hooded top. But that was fine. Mum kept asking me if I liked it and I said I did, which was true, but I don't think she believed me. Then she said that she'd tried to get me an iPod but they'd sold out. I knew this wasn't true but I just nodded my head. Mum's eyes were watering and I was embarrassed. I took my fork and shovelled in a mouthful of sausage roll. I swallowed and took another mouthful. Mum didn't look up. Drips of water from her eyes were landing on her carrots. I only wanted the iPod so I could upload bird songs. But it was ok because I had a CD with a lot of them on. I tried to tell my mum this but she got up and left the room.

When she came back she seemed more together. She took the half empty bottle of wine from the middle of the table.

—Want another Paul?

—Are you sure mum?

—Sod it, it's Christmas.

She filled up both our glasses. We watched the Doctor Who Christmas Special. For some reason, this made mum cry again. I wish I could comfort her, but putting my arm round her doesn't feel right somehow, and I can't think of the right thing to say.

On the television there was a killer Christmas tree, with its arms spinning, approaching the Doctor's assistant, Rose, her mother, and her boyfriend. They were recoiling in horror. It should have been funny, but it wasn't, it was sinister. A distorted Christmas carol played in the background. It sounded demented. The Doctor came round and used his sonic screwdriver just in time. There were all these people standing on the edges of buildings ready to jump off. When the doctor and Rose got ready to go off in the Tardis once more, leaving Mickey and Rose's mum, mum started to cry again.

I spot a cafe and go inside. I order a full English and a mug of tea. I take the tea and sit down. I flick through the paper. There's a small piece about us, but it doesn't say anything on top of last night's report. Good, I think, although it still doesn't mention Ashley. I'm starting to think I will have to make

Ashley disappear. Everything is leading me in that direction. My breakfast comes and I get stuck in. I hadn't realised how hungry I was, but thinking about it, it's over 36 hours since I've last eaten. Toast, fried bread, beans, sausage, bacon, fried egg, half a tomato, black pudding, I leave the mushrooms. I don't know why they give you the mushrooms, no one ever eats the mushrooms. I gulp down the tea. There is a television in the cafe and the news is being broadcast. It's the regional news. The photograph of me appears again, the same photograph as last night. I hide behind the newspaper.

Now they are interviewing the owner of the bed and breakfast we stayed in. —Yeah, that's him alright. He checked in about seven last night. I'd just sat down when I saw him on the news. I rang the police straight away. When I went up to his room, he'd already climbed out of the skylight.

There is a fat man watching the news, shovelling breakfast into his mouth, and an old couple too, drinking tea and chewing toast. I get up and slink out of the cafe. The first thought I have is Dave. Dave will be somewhere not so far away, perhaps a pub in Helvellyn, watching the news as well. Now he knows we are in Carlisle.

I make my way back to the empty house and through the broken door. I walk up the stairs. I enter the bedroom. Ashley is slumped in the corner. He is clearly stoned. I go up to him and shake him.

—We've got to go.

He looks at me without comprehending. I see the opened wrap and a rolled up note. Ashley has snorted the last of the ketamine and is a complete mess, unable to even lift his head.

—Listen, everyone knows we're here, in Carlisle, Dave will too. It's on the news. We've got to go.

I'm hoping some of this will sink in but he's far too mashed to grasp the seriousness of the situation. He just sits staring at the chaotic pattern on the carpet. I've been gone for about forty minutes. I've still not bought credit for my phone, or any breakfast for Ashley, but it doesn't look like Ashley is wanting any. I doubt he even understands what it is. I perch on the end of the bed for perhaps thirty minutes, staring at the heap of human flesh that is Ashley. What to do? Need to get credit for my phone. Need to sort Ashley out. Maybe I don't sort Ashley out. Leave Ashley where he is and Ashley will vanish. Stop trying to carry him, you owe him nothing. Maybe the safest thing now is to go to the police. Best for both of us.

Is he a killer? Or was he provoked. He seemed to like Smiler. Perhaps he realised, like me and Becky did, that he was just a sad loser full of shit. Is that a reason to kill someone? But it's hard to say and he's certainly not in a fit shape to admit it now. It's like that bloke Richard, when I was a kid I thought he was great, couldn't understand why mum didn't want to go out with him, even though I knew she'd stopped going out with men. Then I thought he was attacking women, and I learned he was a vigilante, beating up the dealers in the area, who were at best just desperate smackheads themselves. I didn't like him after that. I realised he was a threat. Maybe Ashley realised that Smiler was a threat. The truth is what you know at the time. I'm thinking through all this when there's a knock at the door. The front door. I freeze. Then I edge over to the window and peep out from behind the curtains. I can just make out two policemen. They stand back and look through the windows. I duck down.

If they come round the back they will see the broken door and come in. I creep over to the window again and have another peek. They have moved onto the next house. A woman comes to the door and they show her a photograph, of Ashley I imagine. They say something to the woman and she shakes her head. She goes back inside and the policemen move on. We can't stay here, that's for sure. If I'm to get Ashley out of here I need to sober him up. I also need to get credit for my phone. The only thing I want to do now is ring Becky. My phone rings but it's just mum so I divert to answer machine. I go out the back way and walk back to the precinct. I buy a triple espresso from a coffee vendor in the square. The magic potion that's going to straighten Ashley out and make him disappear. Perhaps a sausage roll as well. There are more people about now.

I walk across the precinct towards a newsagents that sells top-up cards. As I do I see a blue car pull up at the lights. Dave is in the front passenger seat talking to a man driving and another two men sit in the back looking out of the window. I pull my hood up some more. The lights are still on red. Change. I stand there quite still, hoping no one will notice. Change. They are looking for movement. The lights change and the car pulls away, but as it does, Dave looks back and for a split second, we make eye contact. I see a flash of anger in his eyes. I duck down a side street, spilling the coffee in the process. Need to get a sausage roll.

I carry on up the side street. I get to the end, but there's no way out. I'm surrounded by shops but no way out. I walk back down. As I do I see Dave with the three men pass the entrance to the street. They see me. I chuck the coffee and run through Primark, through the ladies section, up the escalators, pushing people out of the way, to the gents upstairs. I look behind me, Dave and his men are running after me. Where now? I look around. They are making their way up the escalator. I run into a changing room. I watch them move round the store, leaving me just enough distance to run back down the escalator. I wait until they are further away, then I make a run for it. I get to the escalator when I hear one of them shout. I turn round to see them running towards me. Clothes rails tumble and crash. A small child screams. Down the escalator and through the shop. There's a security man and he's coming after me too. I'm running down the street now.

They're catching up. I come out of the street and run across the precinct. Dave and his mates are gaining on me. The security man is behind them. Then I see a police car. I run over to it.

I've never been so pleased to see the police in my life. I tap on the window.

—I think you're looking for me, I say. I pull down my hood. All they've spotted is just another dull brown bird. But they open the back door anyway. I'll do for now until they come across the rarer find.

The Dunnock

The king of the small dull brown birds is surely the house sparrow. No bird watcher I've ever come across has ever welcomed its sight. The truth is they are everywhere. It is one of the most widely distributed wild bird on the planet. There is nothing remarkable about the female at all. At least the male has a distinctive black bib and cap. The female has no black on her head or throat, not even a grey crown. It's almost the complete opposite of me and Becky. House sparrows are cheerful exploiters of our rubbish and waste, so we should cut them a bit of slack.

They are very similar to the tree sparrow, they're both sturdy, thick-billed little birds with similar markings, but nothing like the so-called hedge sparrow. The hedge sparrow isn't a sparrow at all, so I don't know why people persist in calling them hedge sparrows. It is probably the same people who call gulls 'seagulls'. The proper name of the so-called 'hedge sparrow' is the dunnock. It is much more like a robin or a wren, or even a dipper than a sparrow and deserves to be thought of as something better than just a small dull brown bird. Its face and breast are classed as grey, but I think they're a shade of blue, a very subtle and beautiful shade of blue. I'm quite partial to a dunnock.

I'm thinking about this as we park up at the back of the house. All the books I have read describe its breast as grey, but I'm looking at one right now, and I can tell you, it's blue. It's creeping along the floor near a privet. It sort of shuffles about in the shadows, but even without full light, its breast is clearly blue. Probably foraging for insects, spiders, even worms.

One of the policemen has gone into the house. The other sits in the driving seat. I've told them everything. There's a long pause. The radio keeps crackling and a distorted voice cuts in from time to time, but it's difficult to make out what's being said. It can't be anything to do with us, because the policeman just ignores it.

The policeman brings out a still-very-stoned Ashley. He sits him next to me on the back seat and we drive to the station. I still haven't got credit for my phone, but am thinking that you're allowed to make a call when you get to a police station. I've seen it on The Met. We seem to wait for ever in the police station before two plain clothed take me into one of the interview rooms. Ashley has been locked up in a cell. They said they would keep him there until he came round. I told them he'd taken ketamine.

They took his belt off him and his laces and all the drugs. I go with them into the room. They have a recording machine. One of them talks into it. He says the date and time into the recording device. He looks at his watch to check. The questions go round and round. I've asked them if I can make a call, but they've told me not yet. That's not how it happens on The Met, but the men don't look in the mood to discuss this so I don't say anything.

—And where were you when this happened?

—I've already said, I was looking for ravens.

—And you expect us to believe you came all this way to find ravens?

—We were on the run from Dave. It was my idea to come to the Lakes, because I wanted to find some ravens.

And off we go again. I go from the beginning, to the Tower of London and to the clipped wings. They don't believe me about the ravens, but why would I make that up? I've already shown them the book. Then they start asking me about Ashley again.

—It's the truth, whether you believe it or not. I had no idea that Ashley was capable of... of killing someone.

The policeman looks at his notes. —Look, for the third time, who is this Ashley?

—He's my best friend.

—Your best friend?

—Well, he was.

—But he's not now?

—I've told you, he was my only friend, but I don't really know him that well.

The policeman looks at the older policeman. —Paul, we've got the school register here and there is no one by the name of Ashley O'Keefe.

The truth is, I've only actually known him for eight days, maybe he's not registered at the school yet. That hasn't occurred to them. It's an obvious point but not to them. Still, it's not my place to be doing their job for them. I nearly say, he was my only friend until I met Becky, but I want to keep Becky out of this. I tell them it's likely that Ashley killed Smiler in self-defence. I tell him about the shadow-boxing incident, and make it clear that I think he had a screw loose. It turns out the police know Brian Smith. He has a long criminal record, so I don't suppose he was lying about that.

—And where did you meet him?

—Ashley?

—Look, we've told you, we don't know who this Ashley is, we're asking you about Brian Smith.

—In his house.

—You met him in his house?

—Well, it's more of a shack really.

I try and tell them about Ashley again, but they're not having any of it. I want to tell them that he used to remind me of a raven, but I don't because I can see that it would sound stupid. That he reminded me of a raven, then a crow and eventually a jackdaw. He doesn't even remind me of a jackdaw now. He doesn't remind me of a bird at all. Birds can fly except stupid birds such as the penguin who have sacrificed the power of flight in order to live on a block of ice. Ashley can't fly. I thought Ashley could fly but I was wrong.

—There are lots of things that don't make sense.

—I suppose there are.

—You're in a lot of trouble.

—Well, you see, it's Ashley. I had no idea he was so disturbed.

The policeman looks wearily at the older policeman. He sighs. —Ok, let's talk about Ashley. When did you realise he was disturbed?

—Not at first.

—So when?

—I've said, when I found out he'd killed Smiler.

I want to talk to Ashley, but they have kept us separate. He will have probably come round now and I want to tell him not to mention Becky.

—And you say Ashley killed Smiler to attract these ravens?

—That's what he told me. He could have been in shock. I don't think that's the reason.

—That's a strange thing to do don't you think?

I explain my theory again, that Smiler attacked him. I never believed the raven bait story, but why am I wasting my breath on these people?

—When can I make a phone call?

The policeman looks at his colleague and smiles. It's like I've asked a really stupid question. We go through it all again. They make notes. They look back at their notes and ask more questions. In the back of my mind I'm expecting them at some point to give me a beating, but I don't know why, you don't see that on The Met, but I have seen it in films. Which is more truthful, The Met or the films? I hope it's The Met. I've told them about Dave. They've taken my mobile off me, but I've memorised Becky's number. I keep saying it in my head so I won't forget. But they keep asking me questions and I keep thinking I'm going to forget the number.

The policeman takes out the bag of drugs and puts it on the table.

—What about this lot then?

He talks into the recording device explaining that he has just taken out a bag containing what is left of the drugs. Only he doesn't use the word drugs, just describes the contents matter-of-factly. I try to tell him that the bag belongs to Ashley but he's not having any of it. We go round and round, asking the same questions, me giving the same answers. Ashley, Ashley, Ashley. 07789 982558. Keep saying the number in your head. Keep saying Ashley when they ask a question. Ashley. 07789... Keep saying the number in your head. Ashley... 982... Ashley... 558. Like juggling at the same time as riding a unicycle. I've never ridden a unicycle or juggled.

Eventually I get to make my phone call, but it goes straight to answer phone. Why wouldn't she have it switched on? There could be a simple explanation. It's charging up, or she's out of signal range, but the simple explanations keep getting shoved aside in my mind and all I can think about is Dave. I've given the police as much information as I can about Dave, but they don't seem that interested. They're more interested in Ashley.

I keep telling them that it is really important that they arrest Dave, but what has he done that they can arrest him for? This is the problem. They say they don't know anything about Andy, Dave's brother, and they haven't heard of any car accident that fits my description, but he's hardly likely to report it to them. They call me a joy rider. As far as they are concerned, I'm the baddy. I killed Smiler. It is me they are after not Dave.

And then I think about my dad. Maybe mum had good reason to leave dad. Let's face it, if he was a decent bloke, he'd have been in touch by now. As soon as I have that thought I get a chill which runs through my body. It's obvious. He's a bad man. All these years I've had this idea of my dad in my mind. He was the wronged party, he was the good man in the world trying to do good where he could. He was thrown out by mum and he came back but she wouldn't let him in and I've always blamed her for that. But what if he wasn't the goody? What if he was the baddy?

They keep asking me questions and I keep telling them about birds. I tell them about the red-backed shrike and the woodcock. I think I am finally getting through to them. I'm examined and questioned by a psychiatrist. I wonder if Ashley has come round and whether he's in the interview room with the police. I wonder if he's mentioned Becky. What's he going to say? Would he even remember her address? They tell me my mum and sister are in the waiting room. They tell me there is no Ashley. They say I can't go home.

The Pied Wagtail

I actually don't mind funerals. It would be amazing to find a raven at a funeral but of course that isn't likely to happen. It's over a hundred years since ravens lived in our cities. Everyone thinks they are an omen. They use them in horror films and when they do they are always associated with death. We should be really glad to have them at all. I mean where are the other so-called wild animals in this country? Where are the bears, the wolves, the wild boars? We've killed them all off. The truth is we don't like things that are truly wild.

I'm thinking about my time with Ashley as a good thing. It lasted only a week, just over, but we did so much then that I feel like I've really lived now. If I was to die tomorrow, I wouldn't have any regrets, only not seeing Becky. That would be a regret. I wonder if Ashley had any regrets? I'm surprised at how many people are here. They can't have been friends. He didn't really have any. There was Dave and his mates – but you couldn't call them friends. Then I see them, they are here, dressed in white suits with angel wings. Four of them. Andy, only Andy, has blood dripping from his eyes and mouth. He smiles at me and more blood pours out.

No one else seems to have noticed them, this crowd. Perhaps they are the same crowd of people that gather around car accidents. They are just here to watch and be glad it isn't them in that wooden casket. Some of them don't have faces. We're in a sort of hall. It's not a church. Well, it is a church but the building hasn't been built specifically as a church. There are so many people here that they can't all get in. I suppose that's what happens when you die young. My classmates and kids from school make up about thirty percent of the group so god knows who the other people are. I suspect a lot of them are Ashley's family. I didn't realise he had such a big family. It's funny, we never talked about our backgrounds. I didn't really know anything about him at all it seems. It seems he was the oldest of five. Two brothers and two sisters. One of his sisters is still a baby. Both his mum and his dad are here. His mum is crying. As is his older sister.

—Good, the psychiatrist says. She insists I call her by her first name, Kate. We are in a special room designed for one-to-one therapy sessions. It isn't like the rest of the building. There is wallpaper on the walls and comfy furniture. There is a vase of flowers on a pine wood coffee table, but they aren't real flowers. Next to the flowers is a box of tissues.

—The more back story you can create for Ashley the better. In order to grieve for him he has to be fully alive in your mind first. Do you want a break before we carry on?

—It's ok, I say.

—Good, well let's continue. Tell me what happens next.

I start again. —We've all been given a programme, like you get when you go and see a show, only this one has Ashley's picture on. He looks really smart in his school uniform and he also looks really young. What he looks like is a sixteen-year-old boy, which is what he is. Then it says his full name, Ashley Daniel O'Keefe, and the year of birth and death. I guess you could say the ravens were persecuted. No one can withstand that level of persecution without showing some ill effects and there are limits to anyone's resilience. I realise though, despite my sympathies, I am no longer fascinated by them. I've moved on, as they say.

—Good Paul, but your thoughts are wandering again.

I open the programme and there is a list of events. There's this cockney bloke on stage and he has a mike. He cracks a few jokes which don't go down too well. He is talking about his own childhood in the east end of London, he paints a rosy picture – but no one knows him and no one is here to listen to him waffle on about his childhood in London. His head starts to expand and form scars. He is turning into Smiler.

—Let's focus on Ashley, Paul. Brian Smith was a real person. Let's keep the two things separate. She tells me again about this Russian bloke. He was a professional memory man. He could memorise a phone book, he could memorise anything. Only he got so good at it that he lost the ability to forget. He couldn't forget anything. It got so bad that he couldn't recognise his own mother. When he saw her, she just seemed to be made up of still images. The eye is like a video camera, it takes a set of still pictures. It is only because we have the power to forget that we can understand these as a moving image. In the end, the only way this Russian memory man could be cured was for him to write words he wanted to forget on a piece of paper and burn them. That is what we are doing here. I'm burning the memory of Ashley.

We are here to talk about Ashley and then burn his corpse, polluting the air, as the Parsi would say. I don't need to kill off Andy and Dave as they were a product of Ashley. Killing off Ashley will also kill off Dave and Andy.

Things at home are not good. I've been permanently excluded from school. There's a sort of programme for excluded pupils the college runs, which I'm supposed to go to. It's geared towards more vocational stuff. You can do catering or mechanics – a load of other stuff. But I've not been yet, I've got to stay in this place for a bit longer they say. Mum says as soon as I get better, they'll let me out. This is part of me getting better, my doctor's idea. The coroner reported accidental death in the end, which surprised a lot of people. We were told it would be a suspicious circumstances verdict. But an accidental death verdict is better for me.

Mum is moving out soon. Whether I go back to the old house or not will depend on when I get released. I don't mind, we've not been there long enough for me to get attached to it.

—Come on Paul, you can do it. Focus.

Me and Kate have discussed this at length. It's very common to have imaginary friends, she said, but it's not so common for them to carry through to adolescence apparently. Imaginary friends, or imaginary companions, as some psychiatrists call them, are often invented as a form of protection. I extended that role. The thing about people who are there to protect you, is that they are potentially dangerous people. It's like the men on the estate who buy those fighting dogs, pit bulls and rottweilers, and are then surprised when they chew off the face of their kids. Imaginary friends can be exactly like real people. The psychiatrist said that two thirds of school age children have an imaginary companion by the age of seven.

The only other funeral I've been to was my grandma's. I'm basing a lot of Ashley's funeral on that experience. The programme idea, for example. My granddad died before I was born and I don't know about my grandparents on my dad's side – they could be dead, they could be alive. Who knows? My grandma's funeral only had about twenty-odd people, but she was quite old. My mum was the youngest and she'd had her at forty. I didn't really like my grandma. Whenever she took me to the park and I'd talk about birds she'd say —Stop rabbiting on about birds, Paul. Why don't you play football like normal boys?

Mum brought her girlfriend and she made a point of kissing her on the lips. —That'll show the old cow, she said. I don't think mum liked grandma either. She used to judge everyone, and everyone was guilty. She never smoked or had a drink. And she thought this made her better than everyone else.

Mum used to say that granddad died because he'd had enough of grandma. They didn't get on. But they didn't argue either, they just sort of ignored each other.

—Let's get to the end Paul. Let's get to the point we discussed, remember?

Someone has just given a speech and everyone is clapping. Even Dave and his gang clap, although Andy's clap is sloppy due to all the blood on his hands. Ashley's mum is sobbing uncontrollably now. His dad has his arm around her. All his brothers and sisters are also crying. And I notice that I'm crying as well.

When I came here from the police station, I wasn't allowed to see mum for a few days, but when I did at last get to meet with her we had a big talk. She said that Tina had been worried about me, which surprised me, maybe she's not that bad. She switched the telly off in my room, so I knew it was serious. She'd said I was in a lot of trouble, which is what the police kept saying to me, but I don't know what I've done wrong. She told me she had spoken to the headmaster and he had no choice but to permanently exclude me. I'm not bothered about that, though, because I didn't go to school very often anyway. I prefer the library. They've got better books and you don't get distracted. You can actually learn something. It's very easy to get books in here, you just ask for them and then a couple of days later, they're here.

Ashley's mum is wailing now. The cockney man introduces this Christian hymn. I don't know the words but they are projected on a screen above him like in a karaoke bar. I got this idea from my grandma's funeral as well. We all sing along, even me, even though I don't like the song or want to sing along to it, I do, because it seems disrespectful not to. Even though Ashley would have hated the song and wouldn't want me to sing it, it still feels disrespectful. Work that one out.

173

I've been to a lot of schools in my time and they all have one thing in common – they're all rubbish. Three days after my arrest, Becky rang. She said she was sorry not to answer my texts or voicemail messages, but she had a lot of thinking to do. I explained everything, that I'd killed my imaginary friends off. She didn't freak out like I was expecting. It turns out, she had three imaginary friends until she was about ten years old, and even now, when she thinks about them, they seem real, so it's not that weird after all. It's weird to my mum and to my sister, but to Kate and Becky, it's normal. That's the thing about being weird, you are only weird if people say you are.

Becky apologised about thinking I'd killed Brian Smith. She got carried away, she said. But that's ok, I blamed Ashley, so we're both guilty on that front. Some of the crags around Helvellyn are really dangerous, it's really easy to lose your footing. I've still got my own scar on the side of my head to prove that. The police said Brian Smith was an accident waiting to happen. I can't help thinking it was something to do with all the skunkweed he had smoked, which was my fault I suppose, but at the time I couldn't see any other way of persuading him to let us stay. The police didn't think it was my fault. They said that if you drink that much beer and wander round some crags at night, there's a good chance you'll come a cropper. It's no wonder the area is so popular with ravens.

Becky rang a few days after that and asked me to come up and see her in Kendal. So that's what I'm going to do once I've got this funeral over with and they let me out of here. If it ever ends. It's been over thirty minutes and there's no exit sign yet. We're only about two-thirds of the way down the list. There's another hymn coming up, then a prayer, then another hymn and another speaker to get through yet.

Something about Kate is familiar. She's quite old, probably late 30s, tall and thin and has reddish hair. She has her hair tied back but great big curls of the stuff spring free as she talks. She reminds me of a woman I met a long time ago. I was in the park, it was summer. I was with my sister and some of her friends. Mum had made her take me with her, they had shouted at each other a lot, but in the end my sister agreed. We were playing hide and seek. It was a beautiful day. The sun was shining. And I lost them. At first I thought they were hiding, but no, I couldn't find them anywhere. I wasn't that worried, I knew how to get home. I knew the road which would take me home, but I didn't know how to get to the road. And there were a lot of trees, I couldn't really see. I thought to myself, if I go to the edge of the park I'll see the road, and if I see the road, I'll be able to find my way home. So I went to the edge of the park.

It was the wrong road. I went back on to the park and I started to get a bit worried because it was getting late. I wasn't sure what I was going to do. Then I saw this woman and man. A tall, thin woman with wild reddish hair. I don't remember the man. He had glasses on. I remember the glasses. They came up to me and they could see I looked worried. And they asked me what was wrong. I knew I shouldn't really talk to strangers, because my mum had told me never to talk to strangers, but I didn't know what else to do. I was lost. I was in the park by myself. So I told them. They told me not to worry.

The woman said to me, —Would you like an ice cream? And I thought, yeah, that'd be nice. So she got me an ice cream. It was a Screwball with a bubble gum in the bottom. I used to love that bubble gum at the bottom. I chose strawberry flavoured juice. I didn't like chocolate juice, I liked chocolate, but not chocolate juice, but I did like strawberry juice. It was really nice. They said to me, —Come back to our house, we've got a map. We'll get the map out, and we'll find your house, and we'll be able to get you home.

I started walking with them back to their house. I was holding the woman's hand. But then something gripped me. It was fear. Something wasn't right and I pulled my hand from her grasp and ran. They both shouted after me, but I kept running. I ran down the street. I don't know how I found it but in the end, there it was, the road that led back to the estate.

When I come round, things seem to be progressing. We are on the last speaker. Another relative I think. Then we all have to sing another song. Then the cockney man asks us to be silent as the coffin moves along a conveyor belt. But you don't see any flames or anything. As it disappears, I watch a pied wagtail fly past, a flicker of black and white and a sort of undulating flight pattern. It seems to be waving goodbye, though obviously it's not waving goodbye because birds don't understand the wave goodbye. I'm not sure I understand the wave goodbye. What does it mean? Are you shooing someone away? Perhaps we just need a signal that says this is the end. A wave goodbye, it's like you are painting a great big invisible full stop in the sky. I don't understand the wave goodbye but I understand why we need it.

—I know this wouldn't happen in real life Paul, but I want you to see the coffin burn. It's important you witness it.

I do what Kate says. The curtain is pulled back and there's the coffin. Then the flames come from a pit underneath. The coffin catches fire at the corners and the pine-coloured wood darkens. Pretty soon the flames are alive, licking the sides of the box, flickering yellow and orange. The flames grow and darken. The box is consumed by them. It turns black and then starts to glow amber and red. The flames roar and the box crackles and spits. Then the flames die down leaving only embers. The coffin is reduced to just a few charcoal lumps. Even these die down and leave a smoking bed of blackened crumbs. We have burned the box. That's it. Ashley is no more.
    —Well done, Kate says. She pats my knee and smiles. She hands me the box of tissues.

The House Martin

I'm sitting in the front room. There are still boxes of unpacked items scattered around and loose strands of newspaper. The pictures still lean against the wall, waiting to be hung. I'm wondering when mum will get round to actually moving in, but then I think, there's not much point as we are about to get re-housed. Somewhere safe, mum says. Perhaps that's why mum always takes so long to move into a place, somewhere in her mind, she's already getting ready to move out. Mum comes in from the kitchen carrying two cans of lager. She hands one to me.

—Here.

I take the can and open it. I drink from the can.

—How you feeling now? she asks me.

—Ok.

We don't say anything for a while, just sit and drink. It feels like the final drink, like this is it for me and mum. I watch a house martin as it flies back and forward with mud in its mouth as it constructs its nest below the eaves of our house. We did have house martins when we lived on the estate with dad, although not when we had the flat in Ordsall because the eaves were twenty floors up. But the one under the eaves on the estate was quite a well-established nesting site. Only one day the nest fell to the ground with the young still inside. I was quite small at the time and I didn't know what to do, but a neighbour got a pair of ladders and nailed an empty ice cream tub to where the nest had been. He put the damaged nest inside. Miraculously the baby birds weren't injured.

The parents seemed to abandon the new nest, until the cries of the young brought them back. The thing was, mum didn't like the nest. It was just above our door, and the droppings were a problem. She wanted to destroy the nest, but me and my sister protested and in the end she gave in to us. Shortly after that, a sparrow, for no good reason I could make out, damaged the nest. Not only that, it attacked both the adults and the young. Eventually it drove the martins away. And that was the end of that, they never came back, but we still had an empty ice cream tub nailed to the underside of the eaves of our house.

—What's she like?

—Who?

—This girl.

—Becky? She's lovely, mum. She's really lovely.

I try and describe her, but it's hard describing someone. They're not like birds. You can't just give a physical description followed by their habitat and call. You don't really get a sense of a person that way.

—Paul?

—Yes?

—Is Becky real?

—Of course she is, mum.

She wants to know where I'll stay. I tell her I'll stay at Becky's. Becky says her parents are alright about me staying for a few days even though they've never met me. They don't know about the trouble I've been in with the police. They don't watch television, which is good for me as they might think I was a 'joy rider' and what was that other word they used on the telly, a 'delinquent'. I had to look that one up. Apparently it means someone who is 'failing in or neglectful of a duty or obligation'. But I don't have any duties or obligations, except for washing up and putting the bins out, and the only time I failed to do that was when I was in the Lakes. I got the all clear from the psychiatrist – neither a danger to others, or himself. That was her verdict.

I've always been quite happy to wash up. It's a great opportunity to play my birdcall CDs – swot up on them. You need that, something really easy to do while you're listening. I don't mind putting the bins out either. It's an excuse to have a look around. One thing though that I've got from my trip to the Lakes is that there's more to life than birds. Don't get me wrong, I love birds. I love the way they look and I love the fact they can fly, but it doesn't stop there. There are drugs for instance, some of them good, some of them not so good. I quite like smoking dope, and taking ecstasy is lovely, but I don't think I'll be in a hurry to try ketamine again.

It's funny, when I found the bag that day in the cloakroom at Roseway, I really wanted to try them, I'd read so much about them, seen them on the telly, but it was just easier to give someone else the responsibility. Ashley had appeared at a point of danger. I'd conjured him up to protect me. It seemed logical to have him to blame as well. It's the same with stealing cars. I'd watched it so many times on The Met. It looked so exciting, like flying. It seemed to me that stealing a car was the closest I'd get to fly in Salford. So many times I'd played this video I found on YouTube teaching you how to hotwire a car, but when I actually got round to doing it, it was just easier to give someone else the job.

More than any of these things, though, is Becky. It's another form of flying. You have to be brave. A fledgling swift gets one chance. You have to drop into the sky with your arms opened out. Then just trust. Trust the air to have substance. Trust the power of lift. Trust the thing you need, to be who you are. Trusting someone takes guts.

Mum tells me she's got a moving date and she's found out where they're moving her to – The Cliff. She's happy about it. Weaste is not that bad but The Cliff is much nicer, she says. I nod, but I'm more concerned about her use of the word 'me'. She said moving 'me' not 'us', which is a bit disturbing. Already in her mind, she has moved me out. I try and lighten things up and talk about how she won't have to pack any boxes as most of them are still packed up. She smiles and says, —Wait there. When she comes back she has a box in her hand.

—I've been sorting out your stuff. There's a few things we can chuck. Do you want this? she says, and she lays the box between us and opens it. It's my box of bird skulls. I've built up quite a collection over the years.

—I don't mind, I say at last.

—You sure?

—Chuck it if you like mum.

It's not even noon yet, a bit early for the lagers maybe, but it's not as though it's a habit. I don't rush my drink. I sup it slowly. I suppose I'm hoping for a more meaningful conversation, but it doesn't happen. She holds her lager and stares at the blank grey wall. I stare out of the window. There's a web in the top frame and I watch as a spider approaches a fly that it has caught. The fly wriggles in the netting. The spider is much smaller than the fly. It inspects its catch. It doesn't kill it. It starts to wrap it up using its two back legs and the silk from its silk glands. It works quickly, wrapping up its wings and legs, then it flips it over and wraps it up some more. All this takes about three or four minutes. Then it drags it back to its nest. Why doesn't it eat the fly? I'm wondering. It has probably already eaten and it makes sense to keep the fly alive so that it is fresh later on when it feels hunger again.

—The Cliff will be great mum, won't it? I manage to say at last.

She nods.

—Better than Ordsall, I say.

It was a rather stupid thing for me to say, because mentioning Ordsall will remind her of when she had to go into hospital and me and my sister had to go to that place that wasn't very nice. It was during our time in Ordsall that mum went for my sister with a knife. It was during our time in Ordsall that a van came and carted her off into the night. So I suppose there are lots of bad memories there. Still, that's all in the past.

In the end, I finish the lager off and pick up my bag. I put my coat on. Mum walks me to the door and she does something she's not done for a long time, she gives me a hug. She clings on to me for ages until it becomes more than a hug, then she moves away and I walk out the door. I turn around and give her a wave and she waves back and I get that feeling I got that day I'd waved to dad from the top of the climbing frame. I catch a bus that drives down Weaste Road past Roseway School and I notice they've taken the Care Bear off the razor wire. Someone must have seen it on TV perhaps. I'm a bit of a celebrity now. Someone at school has even started a Facebook group in my name, Fans of Paul Cooper. I've never had a fan before, or a friend for that matter. Something Kate the psychiatrist said, people need something to believe in, but it's important you believe in the right things. The bus drops me off close to the motorway and I stand near the lay-by with my homemade sign: Kendal.

Several cars go past. The wind blows and I zip up my jacket. I've got my raven book still in the inside pocket and it digs in to my chest. I unzip the jacket and take the book out, then zip the jacket back up again. I open the book and find the photograph of me and my dad and that stuffed raven. For the first time in many years I decide to turn the photograph over and read what my dad wrote. I turn it over, and there it is: *I'll always be here for you son. Love Dad.* It's strange, but for the first time since I was small, reading the message brings tears to my eyes, but maybe it's just the wind. It does that, it makes your eyes water. I take the book and place it gently on the kerb.

More cars go past. I think about the text from Becky: *can't wait to C U xxx*. I wipe the tears away and smile. It makes me feel warm inside. I take a deep breath, everything is going to be alright, I say to myself. Everything is going to be alright. Everything is going to be alright. Everything is going to be alright. I imagine the words going round in a circle, like they do in Manchester Central Library. I look up and see the rooks circling and I think of Smiler and the ravens. It's funny but for a moment on the moors that day, I did actually think I'd killed him, it's a good job people say I didn't. I watch the rooks get higher and higher and fly off. I hold the photograph aloft and watch as the wind carries it up into the sky. And for a moment I think I can fly. Then I laugh. Of course I can't fly, what was I thinking about? You nutter, I say out loud to myself.

Acknowledgements

Many thanks to Kevin Duffy, Hetha Duffy, Leonora Rustamova, Lin Webb, Jim Greenhalf, David Gill, Paul Magrs and Conrad Williams.